CHAPTER ONE

Jaris Spain turned numb when the girl took her seat in American History I. Goose bumps crawled up his arms like caterpillars. Sereeta Prince was a honey-skinned beauty with glossy black curls making little halos around her face. Jaris had been in love with her since junior high. Now the feelings grew stronger. But Jaris was sure that he was no more to her than the yellowing ivy plant in the classroom. She seemed to look right through him like he was made of plastic wrap.

Jaris felt crushed. At times like these he would remember some of his father's bitter sayings. He didn't want to share in his father's hopelessness. But sometimes it came over him like an onrushing darkness.

"The best dreams always get away," Pop would say. "Just when you think you got it all made, it crashes around your head."

Ms. McDowell, the history teacher, came clicking into the classroom on her red high heels. Most of the lady teachers at Harriet Tubman High School wore comfortable shoes, but Ms. McDowell was a striking young woman. She dressed fashionably. And she was one of the best teachers at the school.

"We've been reading *The Grapes of Wrath* by Steinbeck," Ms. McDowell said, "and now we're going to watch the movie that was made of it."

"Isn't that a real old movie where everybody is jumpy and stuff," Derrick Shaw complained, making a face. "Those jerky old movies give me a headache."

"No, Derrick," Ms. McDowell said patiently, "it's a well made movie."

"I've seen it," Sereeta said, "but I'd love to see it again. The director won an

Outrunning the
DARKNESS

ANNE SCHRAFF

SADDLEBACK
EDUCATIONAL PUBLISHING

SADDLEBACK
EDUCATIONAL PUBLISHING
www.sdlback.com

ISBN-13: 978-1-61651-000-8
ISBN-10: 1-61651-000-5
eBook: 978-1-60291-785-9

Printed in Guangzhou, China
1110/11-57-10

15 14 13 12 11   3 4 5 6 7

Academy Award for the movie. It really makes Steinbeck's book come alive."

Ms. McDowell smiled at Sereeta. "Thank you for your comments, Sereeta. I'm sure the whole class will get a lot out of watching it."

Jaris couldn't help but admire Sereeta's cool, confident voice. Even in junior high she always seemed more mature than everybody else. When she glanced back for some reason, Jaris smiled at her, but she didn't seem to notice. And then he felt foolish for smiling at all. He worried that she'd think he was an idiot or something.

Jaris figured she was looking at somebody else anyway.

After class there was a break, and most of the students headed for the machines. Jaris knew Sereeta's routine. She'd always buy an apple or an orange and take it to the little patch of lawn by the bronze statue of Harriet Tubman to eat it. Jaris kept a respectful distance until she had bought her bright red apple. Jaris bought an apple too.

He had no intention of invading her space, but he did walk slowly by as she nibbled on her apple.

"These are really good, aren't they?" Jaris commented.

Sereeta looked up, smiling. "Yes, sweet and crunchy." Her light brown eyes sparkled. She almost seemed pleased to be talking to Jaris. His heart took a wild leap.

"They're really delicious," Jaris said.

"Yes, that's their name," Sereeta said.

"Really?" Jaris asked. He didn't know one kind of apple from the next. "You mean they call them that?"

"Sure," Sereeta answered. She giggled a little. Was she laughing at him for being stupid about apples. "Don't you ever buy apples in the store, Jaris? They got these little stickies on them telling what kind they are."

"I never noticed," Jaris said. Sereeta was so lovely when she was smiling, even if she *was* laughing at him. Jaris wanted to stare at her, but he was afraid she would

4

resent that. "Uh, Ms. McDowell sure was glad you said good things about that movie we're going to see."

"Yes. *The Grapes of Wrath*," Sereeta said. She seemed to be looking past Jaris now, at somebody else. Still holding her now half eaten apple, Sereeta got up slowly, her whole expression changing. "Excuse me, Jaris," she said. She skipped across the grass onto the sidewalk, and Jaris heard her say, "Hi Marko."

"Hey babe," the boy answered. "Chillin'?"

Marko Lane was a junior at Tubman High too. He was tall and broad shouldered with a flashy personality. Jaris thought he was a phony, but the girls liked him. Jaris had seen Sereeta talking to Marko before, but now she seemed really excited to be with him. Jaris thought about the lame conversation he had just had with Sereeta, and he winced in embarrassment.

Jaris felt flushed and warm. Sereeta would probably laugh with Marko about the whole stupid conversation she'd had about apples with this nerd who was coming on to her. Jaris stuffed his hands into his pockets so hard that he almost broke through the bottoms of them.

"Hey Jaris," Alonee Lennox asked. "You okay? You look like your dog just died." Alonee was cute and friendly, and Jaris had known her all his life. They made block buildings together in Head Start.

"I'm okay," Jaris answered. His voice was grumpy. He had a fine baritone voice, and he had won some awards for regional speech contests. But when Jaris was down, as he often was, his voice rasped like his father's. Like a rusty old hinge screeching for oil. Pop always sounded hoarse as if all his sorrows and disappointments settled in his vocal chords.

"You sure seem down, Jaris," Alonee pressed. "Gotta be something wrong."

"Always something wrong, girl," Jaris said in a snarl. "Like Pop says, if it's not wrong today, it'll be wrong tomorrow."

Alonee laughed. "You're being a drag! And just when I had this exciting news to share with you. But if you're too down in the dumps to hear it, I'll just keep it to my own self."

Jaris couldn't stay in a bad mood for long around Alonee. She was too much like a little kitten jumping on a ball of yarn. "Okay girl, what's the exciting news?"

"Tubman High School is going to put on a new play by some lady from New York," Alonee told him. "Seems like her brother graduated from here a long time ago, and she feels close to us. She wants to do something special for the school. Anyway, it's a really cool play, and there's a part just right for you in there, Jaris." Alonee was breathless when she finished.

Jaris laughed. "Girl, I'm no actor. What're you thinking of?"

"You got such a fabulous voice. You've done dramatic readings like Lincoln's Gettysburg Address. Gave me chills," Alonee said. "I'm telling you, Jaris, this is something you can do!"

Jaris shrugged. Except with close friends like Alonee, Trevor Jenkins, and Sami Archer, Jaris was shy. He was no actor. When he was making speeches, he turned into a different person, but that was a far cry from acting. Still, maybe actors did that too, turned themselves into the characters they were playing. "I'll think about it, Alonee. You got a lot of faith in me."

Jaris didn't live far from Tubman. He rode his bike or jogged home. He lived in a nice neighborhood of single-family homes with nicely kept yards. Still, in the past few years hard times had hit a lot of the families. Several houses had been foreclosed. The windows were boarded up, and the lawns had turned brown. But those houses were the exception.

Across Grant Avenue was a whole other world. People lived in apartments and there was graffiti all over, on the walls, fences, everywhere. Gangbangers roamed at will. The Nite Ryders were the worst, but there were smaller, deadly bands. Some of the kids who lived across Grant attended Tubman High, but few graduated.

As Jaris jogged home, he thought about his father. It was Friday and that was always worrisome. If Pop had a bad day at Jackson's Auto Repair, he didn't come right home. He stopped off for some drinks. Pop hated his job as auto mechanic, even though he was very good at it and he earned excellent money. He called himself a "grease monkey," a name that always angered Mom. She and Pop would argue and Jaris hated listening to them. All evening they would bicker, and late at night they would start yelling. So Jaris dreaded Fridays.

Jaris slowed down his gait and turned the corner to his street. From this far off he could see the family driveway. Jaris took some deep breaths. If it was going to be a good Friday night, Pop's green pickup would already be in the driveway. That would mean he had not stopped for drinks. He would be sitting in front of the TV watching basketball. That was good, very good.

Jaris's father was a tall, lanky man. Jaris figured that when his father was his age, he looked a lot like Jaris. "We're lean and mean, boy," Pop would say when he was in a good mood. He was an LA Lakers fan, and he got really excited when the team was on a winning streak. He was always a little sad that Jaris had no athletic ability. But then he often said, "I was a football star and look where it got me. They called me the 'Little Terror' 'cause I could carry the ball underneath those big men. But in the end I got busted, and my football dreams went down the john, right? So don't sweat it that you're not a jock, boy. You won't get no gripin' from me. No way."

Pop had counted on a sports scholarship to get him into college. He was smart, but they weren't awarding as many academic scholarships in those days. So the career-ending injury blew away all Pop's dreams.

"That's when life first kicked me in the behind, boy," he often said. " 'Here, Lorenzo Spain,' life says. 'You thought you had it made in the shade? Well, it's over, sucker.' I couldn't get over it for a long time. Me and my pals went on drinking sprees. They wanted to make me feel better. Helped too. For a little while." He would always end on the same forlorn note.

Pop's attitude was often dark. And Jaris always felt like Pop's darkness would pull him in someday. Somehow, he thought, he had to outrun Pop's darkness.

Jaris could see the driveway clearly now. The green pickup was not there.

A cold chill went up Jaris's spine. He was walking toward the house now, not jogging. His backpack began to feel heavy. He always knew he couldn't count on any sports scholarships to get him into college. His lack of talent in that area left no room for illusions. So Jaris struggled to make good grades. He expected to make it to college that way. He thought he had a good

11

shot. Right now he had a 3.9 GPA. He figured that and student loans would do it for him.

Jaris walked up the driveway. He could hear music coming from his fourteen-year-old sister Chelsea's room. Jaris walked around the side of the house and rapped on Chelsea's window. When Chelsea responded, he told her, "Hey chili pepper, keep down the noise. Pop is going to be home soon and you know how he likes our music when he's down. . . ."

Jaris and Chelsea's father hated rap and heavy metal. After he'd had a few drinks, he hated all music, but especially rap and heavy metal.

Chelsea smiled and nodded, turning down the volume. Chelsea was not bothered as much as Jaris was by the way their parents argued more and more lately. Her bedroom was not next door to their parents' bedroom, as Jaris's was. She didn't hear as much.

When Jaris walked in the front door, his mother was at the computer. She was a fourth-grade teacher and she loved her work. She was good at teaching too. Jaris was proud of his mother's skills and how she took an interest in her students even outside the classroom. When one of her students was sick and needed a bone marrow transplant, Jaris's mother spearheaded the fund-raising and the search for a matching donor. Both were successful, and now the boy was healthy and striving.

"Hi Mom," Jaris said cheerfully, even though he did not feel cheerful and he figured his mother wasn't in a happy mood either. She had to know, as Jaris did, that Pop's lateness was a bad omen. But Jaris forced his voice to be light and cheerful. Mom always stressed how important attitude was. "Show a happy face" was a kind of mantra for her. Mom got that from her own mother, Grandma Jessie. Grandma Jessie loved to quote people like Ella Wheeler Wilcox, who wrote, "Laugh, and the world laughs with you; weep, and you weep alone." Grandma came up with a lot of old timely quotes that Jaris thought were stupid. But then sometimes he thought it would be better if Pop would fake being a little bit happy.

"Good day, sweetie?" Mom asked in her breezy voice. Mom was thirty-eight and she looked much younger. When she bought liquor for a party, she was often still asked for identification to prove she was old enough.

"All good," Jaris said, going along with the game. He made a B minus in math when he was expecting an A. He was having a terrible time finding an endangered animal to write his big science report on. He had made a perfect fool of himself in front of Sereeta again. He kept seeing her bemused smile and imagining what horrible things she was thinking. "Poor Jaris—what a dork!"

"All good, Mom," Jaris repeated, the words tasting like ashes in his mouth. But Mom smiled gratefully. "Oh sweetie, I'm so proud of you, doing well in school, having nice friends. You are going to be

one of the winners in life. I just know it,"
Mom said.

Jaris headed to his bedroom, unhooking
his backpack. It dropped to the floor with a
leaden thud. He felt like some poor pack
animal dragging his daily load every day,
uncomplaining.

Jaris thought of Mom's words. Was he
one of the winners? Was it already decided?
Was he saved from being in that other
unhappy band, the losers? Who decided
such things? When was Pop sent into the
loser's column? Was Jaris headed there too,
and was Mom too blind to see?

Poor Mom, Jaris thought. She did not
see the ominous signs in her son, the bad
genes of Lorenzo Spain coming to maturity.
Sinister and unseen genes, obvious only in
Jaris's heart. How hard he had to work for
good grades. How quickly a teacher's pen
stroke sent him slipping. How hard Jaris
had tried out for every sport at Tubman and
failed in every one. And Sereeta's scorn.
Sereeta was smart and beautiful. Surely she

knew how to pick a winner, and she didn't pick Jaris.

Sereeta's scorn was all the more painful because she was not a nasty girl. She tried to be kind. A witch would have said, "Fool. You never heard of Delicious apples. Where you been living? Under a bridge?" But not Sereeta. Though laughing on the inside, she patiently explained the stickies on the apples in the grocery store bins.

Jaris glanced out the front window. No sign of Pop yet. He walked down the hall to Chelsea's room, where she was chatting on the computer. Jaris poked his head in the door. "Hey chili pepper, you aren't connecting with strange weirdos are you?" he asked.

"Just my BFFs," Chelsea said.

"Know what, chili pepper? There's a sleazy freshman at Tubman who claims he's one of your BFFs. He's got your picture on his phone," Jaris said.

Chelsea scowled. "Jaris Spain, don't you call Brandon sleazy. Brandon Yates is a nice guy. He's lots of fun and he likes me. We both love jazz too. He's gonna start up a band, and he wants me to sing in it," she said.

"Yeah and Martians are going to land soon and show us how to fix the environment," Jaris said.

"Sorehead!" Chelsea snapped.

"Seriously now, little girl—" Jaris began.

"Don't call me 'little girl,'" Chelsea said, "I'm fourteen!"

"Okay, chili pepper, but Brandon is fifteen and he's a student at Tubman. You're still in middle school, and I just want you to be careful. You're the only little sister I got," Jaris said.

Chelsea softened and grinned. "Okay Papa, I'll be careful. Promise," she said.

Just then they heard the sound of Pop's pickup truck in the driveway. Then the front door opened and slammed. You could tell the mood Pop was in by how hard he slammed the door. Right now the whole house shook.

Chelsea and Jaris exchanged looks.

"I guess Pop had a real bad day," Chelsea murmured.

"Sounds like it," Jaris whispered.

Their parents' voices floated from the living room. Mom had sense enough not to ask Pop if he had a nice day.

"How about you sit down and I'll make you a nice cup of coffee," Mom said cautiously.

"Takes more than coffee today," Pop said. His voice was thick, as if he was talking through molasses. He had stopped for drinks all right. More than a few drinks.

"Still, coffee might help," Mom said. She was grasping at straws, old familiar straws.

"Forget the freakin' coffee," Pop said. His heavy footsteps advanced on the liquor cabinet. He swung open a cabinet door and took down a bottle of whiskey.

"I know you're tired, hon," Mom said.

"That freakin' shop was a zoo today," Pop complained. "Jackson was on my case from the minute I got there. Do this, do that. This jerk needs an oil changed before ten. This fool needs a brake reline. I only got two hands. What am I—an octopus? I felt like busting him in the chops. I thought the devil take the freakin' job."

"I know it's hard," Mom said.

"You don't know anything," Pop stormed. "All you do all day is play games with little kids in an air-conditioned classroom. You don't know what it's like in a hot, filthy garage." His voice grew wavy with sorrow and frustration. "I'm forty-four and I feel like I'm seventy. I'm tired. My back hurts. But what good is it to talk? I'm a grease monkey. It's all I am. It's all I'll ever be. I'll go to my grave as a dirty, stinking grease monkey."

CHAPTER TWO

Chelsea walked over and sat in the rocker next to her bed. She used to sit there a lot when she was younger, with a favorite stuffed animal on her lap. She looked sad but she didn't say anything.

"It'll be okay," Jaris said. "He just needs a good night's sleep." Jaris was getting good at this, saying the comforting little lies, like sugar that made the medicine go down.

"Remember when it snowed in the mountains that February? Remember when we all piled in the car and went up there?" Chelsea said.

"Yeah, sure. We made snowmen and snow angels. It was a big deal 'cause it doesn't snow in California," Jaris said.

"Yeah," Chelsea said. "We never get to see snow so close up around this town. That was such a good day. Remember Pop pulled us up the hill in a sled. Then we came sailing down, and we were all laughing. Pop was laughing the hardest. Do you remember, Jare?"

"Yeah, I remember," Jaris responded.

"What were we then, six or seven or something?" Chelsea asked. Her eyes were wide and moist. "On the way home we got burritos. They were the best burritos I ever had."

"Yeah, Chelsea, you just turned five that winter. I was seven. It was a great day," Jaris said.

"Maybe we could go someplace this summer, some fun place," Chelsea said. She wanted to bring back the emotions of that day in the snow, when everybody was happy and laughing.

"Yeah, maybe," Jaris responded, but he didn't believe they could recover the joy of that time with a vacation.

Chelsea kept some of her stuffed animals on her bed. A raggedy light brown bear had always been her favorite. She reached for it now and held it in her arms. She didn't seem fourteen years old anymore. Jaris bent over and kissed the top of her head, on her reddish brown curls. Chelsea was the only one in the family with red in her hair. Mom told them once that way back they had a Scottish ancestor with red hair, and his genes must have found their way to Chelsea. "Take it easy, chili pepper," Jaris said before going to his own room.

The Spain house grew quiet then. Pop went to sleep on the sofa. He wouldn't change his dirty, greasy clothes. He wouldn't shower. He wouldn't come to bed. Tomorrow Mom would call the rug and upholstery cleaners to get the grime off the sofa.

Jaris heard his mother on the phone in his parents' bedroom. He couldn't hear what she was saying, but he knew she was talking to Grandma Jessie. Mom did that whenever there was trouble with Pop. Jaris hated that she did that. His family problems were none of Grandma Jessie's business. She never liked Pop anyway. She was always reminding Mom that she had warned her things would turn out badly if she married Lorenzo Spain.

Jaris had a part-time weekend job at a little chicken place, called the Chicken Shack, on Grant Avenue. Most of the customers were elderly people from the good side of the avenue, but there were also rough kids from the projects and some Tubman High students, Jaris's friends.

One elderly couple who came regularly, the Joplins, were in their eighties. They both had white hair and twinkling smiles. Mrs. Joplin needed a walker, but she made a joke of it. She named it "Willie Walker," and she always scolded it. "Get going Willy Walker, I ain't got all day," she chuckled as she pushed it along. Her husband would pretend he was shocked. "It ain't enough she bad mouths me all the time, she gotta harass poor Willie too," he'd say with a grin. Then she'd be right back at him. "You shut your mouth, old man." Then she'd look at Jaris, "That man of mine got less sense than Willie," she'd say. Then they would order their favorite, the Asian chicken salad.

Jaris watched them make their way to one of the little tables, where they'd sit and laugh together. He wondered how these two old people continued to be happy and in love with each other even though they were frail and poor. One time Jaris asked the Joplins what their secret was.

They looked at one another. "We got a secret?" Mrs. Joplin said in wonderment.

"Nobody told me about no secret," Mr. Joplin said.

"Lots a time I wanted to be rid of that old man but he never would go," Mrs. Joplin said.

"She say that," Mr. Joplin said, "but truth is she so crazy about me she can't get enough of me."

They ate their Asian chicken salad that day. Then, as they were leaving, Mr. Joplin drew close to Jaris and whispered, "It's her kisses, boy. Keeps a man wanting more." Then, with Mr. Joplin whistling, they walked home together.

Jaris worked until five in the afternoon. About thirty minutes before quitting time, a group of boys from Tubman arrived. One of them was Marko Lane, and he was loud as usual. "She's going with me Saturday night. A beach party and what's gonna go down is gonna be hot, bros."

"Man, you flying high," one of the boys said. "That girl is amazing. She so hot she burns your eyeballs just looking at her. How'd you pull it off?"

"I'm pretty hot myself," Marko said. "I'm like my Daddy. He's got more babes than a mess of cats have lives. All he's got to do is rattle those gold chains around his neck and the ladies come a' running."

"Yeah," one of the others said, "I see that man strutting around town like some big rap star."

Jaris felt his blood boil. He knew Marko was bragging about his upcoming date with

Sereeta. She meant no more to him than the core of an apple he just wolfed down. His father was the big game hunter in the neighborhood, with ladies dangling from his arms, and Marko was gaining the same rep around Tubman.

Jaris knew it was stupid to take Marko on. He should have just kept his mouth shut. But his anger was flooding out his common sense. "Hey Marko, your Pop ever come home and slip your Mama a few bucks? She's a real hardworking lady. It's no fun cleaning other peoples' houses. Maybe your Daddy should sell some of those gold chains and help the family with the groceries," Jaris blurted out.

The boys with Marko looked stunned. Hardly anybody took Marko on. One of them nodded a little. It was a cold thing for a father to be out partying while his wife and kids scrounged for money.

Marko turned on Jaris with a furious stare. "Hey, skinny little nobody. Who give you the right to dis my Daddy? My Daddy's a player. So what? Everybody likes him. Everywhere he goes, they want to buy him drinks. Now your old man has to pay for his own. And from what I hear he ain't no prize," Marko said.

"My Pop works hard and takes care of his family, man," Jaris said. "He goes to work every day, and he pays the mortgage and puts groceries on the table. He pays for our health insurance, and he puts money away for me and my sister to help us when we want to go to college. Maybe he's not Mister Charm, but he's a real man because that's what a real man does. He takes care of his family."

Marko glared at Jaris for another minute before a nasty grin broke on his face. "Hey, you know what put hot sauce in this skinny little dude's underpants?" Marko asked. "Bros, he's got the hots for Sereeta too, and it burns his butt that she chose me and not him. So, deal with it, sucka!"

Jaris said nothing, but Marko and his friends knew it was the truth. Jaris was in love with Sereeta. Marko put his hands on the counter and yelled into Jaris's face, "Tell you what, skinny little bro. On Monday I'll tell you all about Sereeta and how she showed her love for me. I'll give you all the details. I might even text you before that with some of the juicy stuff. So eat your heart out, fool." Marko and the others grabbed their drinks and their supersized chicken sandwiches and strolled out into the late afternoon.

Jaris broke into a cold sweat. Sereeta was book smart and intelligent, but when it came to boys she was naïve. Jaris couldn't let Sereeta get in over her head.

After work, Jaris texted Trevor Jenkins. "Got 2 C U man. Coffee Camp in 10."

The Coffee Camp was a special hangout for Jaris and his friends. They served cheap lattes and regular joe. It was stuck behind a thrift store.

Trevor Jenkins was Jaris's closest friend. Jaris and Trevor started first grade together. Trevor was a troublemaker, the kid who smeared paint on the walls and kicked over the block castle the good little children had built. Trevor threw orange juice at the teacher. He cursed the psychologist who was called in to help him with his ADD—attention deficit disorder. Trevor's mother, Mickey Jenkins, was like most of the mothers in the projects. She had no husband, but she had more courage than some armies. Her husband ran out on her, but she was determined to raise her four boys to be good men.

"Attention deficit disorder," she yelled, "that's bull poop. My boy is just bad. He's baaad and I'm going to cure him of that. I'm going to whup him upside and downside and make him mind. I done it with the three other boys, and they were worse. Trevor is the baby. I'm telling you, nothing wrong with this boy that can't be cured by warming his behind good."

Mickey Jenkins bullied Trevor's older brothers into becoming decent students.

Now two were in the U.S. Army and one was in a community college. Trevor was still wild, but he was earning a lot of Bs at Tubman. To Jaris, Trevor was the big brother he never had. For Jaris, Trevor was the guy who had his back.

Trevor met Jaris within eight minutes.

"Man," Jaris said, "this creep Marko was laughing it up at the chicken place about how he was going to have fun with Sereeta Saturday night. I'm afraid he's gonna try to get her drunk or something, and who knows—I'm so scared she's gonna be hurt bad."

Trevor shook his head. "Dude, you're still into that girl and she can't see you for nothin', man! Can't you get your brain wrapped around the truth, man? She's not having any of you. She's into bad boys like Marko," Trevor said.

"No, Trevor, you got her wrong. She's kind of mixed up. She's a nice girl. Her parents had this bitter divorce, and she really got messed up. Now she's looking for something and she doesn't know what. You gotta help me, Trevor. If I try to talk to her about what a creep Marko is, she's gonna think I just want to be with her and I resent him dating her. I'm going to come off like a bad loser. She won't listen to me," Jaris said.

"Mmmm, let's see," Trevor said. "We could put a bee in Mrs. Prince's bonnet. You know, warn the Mom that her little girl is swimming with sharks."

"No," Jaris said. "Her Mom is married to this new dude. Sereeta is a stepdaughter. Her Mom is more into keeping the new dude happy than looking out for Sereeta."

Trevor screwed up his face. "Jaris, my man, this is a job for Sami Archer. It's bigger than the both of us. We gotta text Sami."

In about fifteen minutes Sami Archer appeared at the Coffee Camp. She was a big girl in extra large jeans and a T-shirt that read, "Don't tread on me, sucka." She had a mane of wild dark hair tied with shiny red

31

ribbon. Her eyes were big and bright, and they pulled you in like magnets. She was supersized beautiful. "What's going down, bros?" she asked over a latte.

Jaris explained the problem. Sami smiled sympathetically. "Poor baby," she said, patting Jaris's cheek. "You're crazy for that chick. She's the cherry on your vanilla ice cream. Well, I feel for the little sister. She ain't bad. She's gorgeous, but she ain't stuck up. I give her that. She got a stepdaddy she don't know from Adam that her mama got off the Internet. She got a mama that don't want to play mama bear like she should. So I feel for the sister. I got me a real mama and a real daddy, and I know what she's missing. So I'm gonna help the poor little fool before she gets her feathers singed."

Sami pulled out her cell phone. "Hey Sereeta? Yeah, it's Sami. The supersized girlfriend. I got a word to the wise, sister. This fool Marko Lane, he's spreading your name all over town and it ain't pretty.

He's saying on Saturday night he and his buds are gonna have you for lunch 'cause you are easy pickins', girl," Sami said. "You hear what I'm sayin'?"

Sami was silent for a few minutes listening to Sereeta. "This is no lie, girl. Listen up. I got no skin in this game, you hear? I just heard these fools bragging on the Saturday night party. On Monday you gonna be the talk of the school. No dog of mine runnin' in this race, Sereeta. I'm not the type of girl who'd get a look from Marko Lane. Not that I'd want that piece of trash. My daddy is a garbage collector. He's proud of helping keep the neighborhood clean. He's an important man. If he comes across Marko Lane, he might just throw that boy in the bin with the rest of the trash. But you do what you want, girl. I'm just trying to help a sister," Sami spoke into her phone. "I'm thinking we girls have to stick together and look out for each other."

When Sami hung up, Jaris asked, "You think you got through to her?"

"Yeah," Sami said, smiling. She had a lovely face. Most people said she'd be really pretty if she lost some weight, but Jaris thought she didn't need to lose a pound to be beautiful.

"I owe you, Sami," Jaris said.

"Don't worry about it, boy. I'd do it for any sister. Some good men around and some good boys at Tubman. My daddy is one of the good ones. Every woman should be lucky as my mama. Marko Lane is one of the sewer rats. Too many of them around. They're not just here in the 'hood. They're all over. Well, I'm glad to be the big old cat sniffin' out this particular rat and warning a sister off."

Jaris hoped Sami had convinced Sereeta to break her date with Marko. Some kids made fun of Sami because of her loud voice and weight. But most of the kids at Tubman liked and respected her. She had a strong street cred. She could help somebody out of trouble or make the best of a bad situation. With the help of her uncle who was a police officer, she turned several incidents around where the culprit got a big time talking to rather than being booked. Sami made good grades too. When she finished at Tubman, she was heading to the community college and then to the state college. She wanted to make her parents proud. Jaris figured she would.

On Monday morning at Tubman, Jaris looked for Marko and his friends. Usually they came swaggering in late to English I, trying to create the most disruption. Mr. Pippin, the English teacher, was not very good. He was desperately trying to last until retirement. He was thin and gray and terrified of his students, especially of Marko and his friends. Mr. Pippin reminded Jaris of a thin little bird with tattered feathers clinging to a tree limb. Eyes wide with terror, waiting for the next gust of wind.

Alonee Lennox and most of the girls filed into class, dutifully carrying their binders. Jaris was one of the few boys who was respectful and quiet, taking notes in class. Studying hard and playing it straight made a boy like Jaris seem like a fool in the eyes of many Tubman students.

"You such a good little boy, Jaris Spain," Marko mocked Jaris back in ninth grade. "You ought to sit with the girls 'cause you're such a prissy little teacher's pet."

Mr. Pippin put his battered briefcase on his desk. He looked around nervously. Jaris could tell by his pale, darting eyes that he was hoping against hope that Marko and his companions wouldn't make it today. That would make all the difference between a decent class and chaos. But it was not to be. As Mr. Pippin launched into a hopeless effort to make nineteenth-century poetry relevant to a bunch of sixteen- and seventeen-year-olds, the door crashed open, admitting the barbarians.

Marko and the three others came stomping in. Jaris figured this is what it might have been like in the Roman senate centuries ago when the Visigoths and the Vandals destroyed Rome. Big, muscular men, boorish creatures laughing and nudging each other, pretending to stumble as they kicked backpacks down the aisle.

Alonee leaned over and whispered to Jaris, "Isn't it pathetic that Mr. Pippin just puts up with this?"

"Yeah," Jaris whispered back, "he's scared."

Mr. Pippin said in a high-pitched voice, "Boys, will you please take your seats?"

Marko grinned and picked up his chair, almost hitting another student over the head with it. His companions followed suit. "Where should we take them, teach?" Marko asked in a mocking voice. Half the class laughed in appreciation. This circus was far more interesting than Mr. Pippin's lectures.

"Marko, I insist you sit down and be quiet," Mr. Pippin said in an almost pleading voice. "You are very fortunate that I am not sending you down to the vice principal."

"Oooooo, thank you, Mr. Pippin," Marko continued in his mocking tone.

He finally sat down, propping his feet on the chair ahead of him. Then he spotted Jaris. He grinned and whispered, "That Sereeta is one awesome party girl, even when she's stoned!"

A wave of nausea swept over Jaris. He had been sure Sereeta would not have gone ahead with the date after what Sami had told her.

"You're a big liar, fool," Alonee Lennox said. "Me and Sereeta and some other kids saw a movie Saturday night. She said she told you she had a headache because she didn't want no part of your freakin' beach party."

Jaris breathed a deep sigh of relief. He grinned in gratitude at Alonee.

The rest of the class was the usual nightmare. Marko and the others baited Mr. Pippin at every turn. They coughed deliberately and made yawning noises, stretching their arms to stress their boredom. Jaris saw beads of perspiration on Mr. Pippin's face. Jaris was angry at the teacher for staying in a job he clearly could not handle, but Jaris felt sorry for the man too. When he began teaching forty years ago, students were not like this. Even the gangbangers showed a little respect to the teacher.

Ms. McDowell would not tolerate this for a second. She would kick the troublemakers out of her class. Mr. Max in speech and most of the other teachers had reasonably good discipline. But Marko and the others sensed weakness in Mr. Pippin, and, with the unerring eye of cowards, they bullied the vulnerable man.

But Mr. Pippin knew he had lost the class, lost the will to teach, lost everything but marking off on the calendar the weeks before retirement. He was serving time, much like a convict in a prison. This classroom at Tubman High had become his cell, and, like other condemned men, he was marking Xs on the wall and living for the day of liberation.

At the morning break, Jaris split a blue-berry muffin with Alonee. "What a waste that class is," Alonee moaned. "I don't think I took one note. And I love old poetry. It just makes me sick how we're being cheated."

"Alonee, how come you and Sereeta went to the movies on Saturday night?" Jaris asked.

"Oh, she called me and told me Sami Archer said Marko was telling everybody sleazy stuff about her. So she cancelled her date with him. Sereeta was really ticked off. So I said me and some girls were going to see this new movie about aliens, and she said she'd like to come along. We had a lot of fun," Alonee told Jaris. "Sereeta is pretty smart, but right now her head isn't on straight. She never would have agreed to date Marko if she was thinking straight. But her Mom is so into this dude she just married that poor Sereeta is the odd man out in her house. Sereeta got desperate and thought why not date this creep even though he's got a bad rep. It's like maybe she was wanting to spite her mother by doing something dangerous and stupid, but the sad part is her mother doesn't care."

CHAPTER TWO

"Poor Sereeta," Jaris said. He remembered Sereeta back in junior high when her
parents split up. Sereeta would sit off by
herself and cry almost every day at lunch.
Then her mother started dating and she got
a guy off the Internet, and they were
married in six weeks.

When Jaris heard his own parents
bickering, he was haunted by Sereeta's
experience. Grandma Jessie had already
brought up the possibility that her daughter's marriage might not survive. Jaris
heard her say to Mom, "Just because that
man has ruined seventeen years of your
life, baby, is no reason to let him ruin the
rest of it. You're young yet, Monica. You
are beautiful and intelligent. You deserve a
man way better than Lorenzo Spain."

Jaris knew it would tear him up inside if
his parents divorced, but it would hurt
Chelsea even more. She was only fourteen.
Sereeta was thirteen when her parents got
their divorce. Chelsea loved Pop as much
as she loved Mom. It made Jaris sick to

think of Chelsea going through the kind of pain Sereeta did.

Sereeta used to take her lunch to the far corner of the brick wall at Marshall Junior High, but she would not eat most of it. She would sit there crying until her beautiful eyes were red and swollen.

Alonee munched on her half of the muffin. "You really like Sereeta, huh Jaris?" she asked.

Jaris shrugged. "Yeah, sorta." He tried to be cool about it but not much got past Alonee. "I've always sort of liked her, but she's not interested in me. I'm not cool enough."

Alonee smiled. "You're one of the coolest guys I know, Jaris," she said.

Jaris felt his skin grow warm. He knew Alonee was just trying to be nice. That's the kind of person she was. She was one of the few people Jaris knew who tried to be kind to everybody. "Thanks Alonee," Jaris said, "but I've got a problem making conversation, especially with girls."

"You do okay with me," Alonee said.

"Yeah, well . . ." Jaris smiled sheepishly.

"Have you signed up for the play tryouts yet, Jaris?"

"Uh no . . ." Jaris admitted.

"Sign up!" Alonee cried when the bell rang for the next class. "That's an order!"

"Okay, okay, I will. That's a promise," Jaris said. He spotted Sereeta walking in his direction. They would both be going to history. It was the only class they shared this semester. Sereeta was wearing a beautiful yellow pullover sweater. It looked so good against her skin. It gave Jaris goose bumps to look at her.

"Hi Jaris," Sereeta said.

"Did you, uh . . . have a nice weekend?" Jaris asked because he didn't know what else to say.

"Yeah, we saw a really hysterical alien movie on Saturday. I was all alone at my house on Sunday. I rented an old Audrey Hepburn movie—*Roman Holiday*. It was great. I just love Audrey Hepburn. She was

43

so amazing. And then she did all kinds of charitable work too. I've seen all her movies. I'd like to be like her. I mean, I'm not nearly as pretty as she was but—" Sereeta was still talking when Jaris interrupted her.

"Yes you are," he said fervently. "You're the most beautiful girl I ever saw." Jaris knew he was babbling like a silly fool, but he couldn't help himself.

CHAPTER THREE

Oh wow!" Sereeta said, her eyes seeming to lock on Jaris's eyes. "That's so sweet, Jaris." For just a second Jaris felt as if he was walking on air. He felt as if he had been launched into space without even the need of a spaceship. He was flying among the stars. He felt as if he could look down and see the entire world, the green forests of Africa, the cities, the vast oceans.

But then Sereeta spoiled it all by saying, "You're such a sweet boy, Jaris. You remind me of my cousin Eugene. He's sweet as sugar too."

Jaris sank like a stone from his grand heights. He had met Sereeta's cousin Eugene. He was a total nerd. He wore huge round glasses. He was a stuffy little twit who kissed up to everybody.

"That's how Sereeta sees me," Jaris thought, wallowing in his misery. He skulked into history, glad they would be watching *The Grapes of Wrath*. He wanted to sit in the darkness to lick his wounds. He wanted to see the gloomy black-and-white images of miserable people during a terrible time in history. He could identify with their despair.

"Sereeta doesn't see me as somebody interesting, some guy a girl might eventually like to date," he thought. "No, she sees me as a sugary little dork like Eugene."

The movie flickered on. A gaunt-faced man was taking his hungry wife and children away from the dust-storm-choked lands of the Midwest westward to California. Everybody in the movie looked sad and hopeless—like Jaris felt.

Jaris stared, unseeing, at the screen. His father's dark words echoed and reechoed in his mind: "The best dreams always get away." The words were like a mantra, relentlessly sounding in Jaris's brain. He fought against them, but they were lodged there because he feared what they said was true. Jaris felt the darkness closing in.

Jaris focused on Sereeta, the object of his hopeless affection. His sadness grew larger, like a throbbing beehive. It buzzed madly in his brain. Slowly, Jaris's other fears mixed with the belief that he would never win Sereeta, even for a date. He thought of his parents' floundering marriage, his own uphill battle to make good grades, and his shyness like an obstacle in the road, always tripping him up.

It was all too much. Jaris felt as if he were choking as the dramatic music from the movie swelled. And then the lights went on.

"Well," Ms. McDowell said, "it was a powerful film, wasn't it? As we read *The Grapes of Wrath* I think we'll all appreciate the book more."

Jaris went through the rest of the class like a zombie. He went home after science, and, as he headed for the street, Alonee called to him. "Did you sign up for the tryouts?" Alonee grabbed his arm. "You haven't got much time. Go and sign up now."

Jaris turned. It was unusual for him to be angry, but now he was. "I'm no actor," he snapped. "Why should I put my name in? I'm just some jerk."

Jaris's brusqueness might have turned off somebody else, but not Alonee. "The play is based on the book *A Tale of Two Cities* by Charles Dickens," she explained. "One of the characters is a guy named Sydney Carton. He's really a gloomy dude. I can see you playing him, Jaris."

"I told you—I'm not an actor," Jaris protested.

"Not yet, but if you don't try out, then you'll never know what you might have been—what hidden talents you never discovered in yourself," Alonee said.

"Oh okay! I might as well make a complete fool of myself and sign up for an audition," Jaris said. He stomped off toward the auditorium, where the drama teacher, Mr. Wingate, was sitting. Jaris never had him in class but heard he was good. He was about fifty but still very handsome with a thick mane of curly salt-and-pepper hair. His classic features were striking. He had been an actor in small off-Broadway productions, but he never reached the stardom he had hoped for.

When Mr. Wingate saw Jaris, he said, "Do you want to sign up for an audition?"

"I guess so," Jaris said. "I'm no actor but some friend of mine has been nagging me to try out. I mean it's a stupid waste of time but—"

Mr. Wingate cut into Jaris's words. "Yes, you're right young man. It is a stupid waste of time for you to try out for this play. Many students are really interested in being a part of an exciting new project. They are hoping for a chance at even a small role. You have such a negative attitude that it would be ridiculous to even sign up."

Jaris was shocked. He didn't think he could feel any worse than he already did, but Wingate had pushed him over the edge. "Fine, goodbye," Jaris grumped, stalking out. He would tell that little Pollyanna, Alonee, that Mr. Wingate agreed he had no chance and threw him out of the auditorium. That ought to end her pressure.

"Oh, just one more thing," Mr. Wingate added. "You're Jaris Spain, aren't you? You have a very fine voice. If you ever get over your rotten attitude, you might want to look into a career that would use that voice to good advantage."

Jaris didn't know what to say; so he said nothing and headed home. He wouldn't jog home today. He wasn't that anxious to get there.

As Jaris walked, he heard a familiar voice behind him. He hadn't heard that voice since his freshman year at Tubman. "Hey Spain, that you?" the boy hollered. "If it's you, you sure got taller than I remember."

Jaris turned. "B.J.? Hey man where

you been hiding?" Jaris asked. The boys high-fived one another. B.J. Brady was a wisecracking troublemaker in ninth grade. Everybody liked him, though, including Jaris. But he was failing in all his classes, and he was using drugs. He dropped out in the middle of ninth grade. He was older than most of the other students, almost sixteen. His parents were trying tough love to turn him around. So they threw him out of the house when he ditched Tubman. They thought he would be so scared he'd come crawling back, ready to obey the rules. Instead, he vanished into the streets.

"Haven't seen you in a dog's age, man," Jaris said.

"I went to 'Frisco, LA, Texas for a while. Man, I even hung out in big ditch with some other dudes once," B.J. said. "How about you, Jaris? Still banging your brains out here at the factory?" He called Tubman High "the factory."

"Yeah," Jaris said. "Sometimes I think I'm crazy, but I'm still hangin' in there."

"I found a sweet spot, man," B.J. said. "I'm not sorry I busted out of here. No way. I used to hate to get up in the morning, come down to school, get reminded how stupid I was. Then go home, Mom and Dad telling me what a big disappointment I was."

"You got nice threads, man," Jaris said. He couldn't honestly say B.J. looked good except for his expensive clothing. His eyes looked strange. He looked wasted.

B.J. peeled out a wad of money. They were all hundred dollar bills. Jaris's eyeballs popped. "Whoa!" he cried. B.J. laughed and said, "Pretty good for a guy not nineteen yet, eh?"

"Is it legal?" Jaris asked.

"Ain' no big thin'," B.J. said. "I been in the dark too long to complain about the sunshine, man. I'm cool, Jare. Any time you get sick of the factory, come see me. Go to Papa's Pool Hall, and they'll know where to find me."

"Well," Jaris said, "good luck to you B.J." Jaris didn't have the street smarts to know everything about the underground economy, but he knew B.J. was swimming in very polluted water to make that kind of money.

"Always room for a guy like you in our enterprise," B.J. said.

"Thanks," Jaris answered him, feeling sad. He liked B.J. Jaris had hoped he'd landed on his feet in a good place, but the streets got him and ate him up. And B.J. didn't even know what had happened to him.

The boys hugged one another and B.J. was off. Jaris stared after him, remembering the old days. When B.J. was ten and Jaris was eight, B.J. taught Jaris some moves on the skateboard that were awesome. B.J. was a good friend. They had some great times together. Jaris hated to see B.J. go when he ditched Tubman.

It wasn't only the grades B.J. couldn't, or wouldn't, make. B.J. was small for his age, and the other kids called him "stupid runt." B.J. was too old for ninth grade and that stung him too. He was a round peg in a square hole.

Jaris thought about losers and winners again. He wondered when the teams really formed up. Was B.J. already a loser in first grade? Jaris couldn't remember. Was there ever a chance B.J.'d get into the winner's column? Jaris's pop seemed to be in the winner's column. He made good grades and was in line for an athletic scholarship. Then he busted his leg and his whole life changed.

Jaris wondered if a cluster of bad things happening can tip the scales and put somebody in the loser's column. When your parents stop loving each other—when hope dies, even the small flickering hope that everything will be okay. When a girl you've loved for almost all your life makes it clear you could never mean much to her.

Jaris sat down on the curb halfway home. In a few seconds a pigeon came along, a blue and gray pigeon with eager, beady eyes. His little head bobbed back and forth. In his pigeon brain, he must have wondered if this creature sitting on the curb might feed him. Jaris would have, but he didn't have anything for the bird. The pigeon marched away on his little orange feet. Jaris had a crazy thought. He wished he were a pigeon. Pigeons had it easy. There was no such thing as a loser pigeon or, for that matter, a winner pigeon. There were just pigeons. If they got to eat and fly, they were winners. If not, they died and that was okay too.

Jaris got up finally and continued on his way home. As he neared his house he saw his father's pickup in the driveway. That was a good thing. His pace quickened. As he drew closer, Jaris noticed his pop had just finished mowing the lawn. Lately he'd been neglecting the yard. "Hi Pop," Jaris said eagerly. "Lawn looks good. Smells good too when you've just mowed it, huh?"

Lorenzo Spain turned and looked at his son. "It needed cutting. Was looking like a jungle," he said.

"Yeah," Jaris agreed. His father seemed in a good mood. "Hey Pop, did you ever read *A Tale of Two Cities*? Dickens wrote it, this guy Charles Dickens. He wrote that Scrooge story too."

"I know who Dickens is," Pop said in a faintly aggrieved voice. "Just because I'm a grease monkey doesn't mean I haven't read anything."

"Sure Pop, I know that," Jaris said softly.

"Yeah, I read *A Tale of Two Cities*. I read all those great books. That one was really good, about the French Revolution and how they chopped heads off," Pop went on. He seemed pleased to be having this conversation with his son. He seemed surprised that he was talking about something important with Jaris. But Jaris was nervous. He didn't want to say the wrong thing. Pop was really touchy.

"They've made a play out of the book and it's going to be at Tubman. Alonee thinks I should try out for it, but I don't know. I've never acted before. I just wondered what you thought, Pop," Jaris said.

Pop stopped raking up the lawn clippings. He took on a thoughtful expression. "I always thought you had a fine voice, Jaris. When you won those speech contests, you put a lot of emotion into the material. It was like acting. Yeah, I think Alonee is onto something. Go ahead and try out. Alonee sees something in you. Go for it, boy."

"Okay Pop," Jaris said. "I'm glad you feel like that. Alonee thinks I'd make a good Sydney Carton. Who was he in the book, do you remember?"

Jaris's father smiled a little. "Oh, that would be a great part for you, Jaris. This fellow Carton was kind of a sad sack. He was a lawyer, but he'd let his life go sour. He loved this girl, but she loved somebody else. Well, in the end he did a very brave thing. He died in place of the man his girl loved." Excitement filled Pop's voice. He was more animated than Jaris had seen him in a long time. "At the end of the story he makes this beautiful speech about doing something better than he has ever done. He was on his way to the guillotine—you know what that was . . ."

"Yeah, the thing they used to chop heads off," Jaris said.

Pop closed his eyes as if remembering something from long ago. "It is a far, far better thing I do, than I have ever done; it is a far, far better rest that I go to, than I have ever known . . ."

"Wow Pop, you remembered that whole quote. You've kept it in your mind for all that time," Jaris exclaimed. "I'm impressed."

"I was good in English," Pop said. "I made all As. I loved English and math too. I loved the sciences." Slowly the excitement drained from Pop's voice. Weariness claimed his face. His shoulders sagged and he shook his head. "See, I didn't care all that much for sports. I was good at baseball, basketball, but I saw them as means to an end. They were going to get me into college. They were the keys. That's what I wanted more than anything."

"I guess there weren't as many scholarships and student loans then, huh Pop?" Jaris asked.

"Financial help wasn't what it is today. That's why when I hear some of those politicians saying we need to cut the money for students, I could wring their necks. If a kid has the desire to go to college, there has to be a way," Pop's voice trailed. He shook his head again. He looked old. He looked fifty or sixty maybe. But he was only a little past forty. He turned then and grasped Jaris's shoulder. "Boy, you go after that part. I'd really get a kick out of seeing you in the play. You give it your best shot, okay? Don't let any chance pass you by. They don't come around every day in the week."

"Sure Pop, I'll do it," Jaris promised. His own spirits were lifted. At that moment, Pop seemed more himself, like in the old days. It was getting a glimpse of him ten years ago. He seemed to get a real charge out of Jaris's coming to him for advice. Jaris felt a little guilty when he realized he wasn't doing that too often lately. He was accepting the fact that Pop was bitter and out of touch and he didn't have much to offer.

The next day Jaris went to see Mr. Wingate again. "Mr. Wingate," Jaris said, "I want to apologize for how I acted yesterday. I was having a bad day. But that's no excuse for being rude like I was. I'm sorry. I talked with my father about being in this play, and he said I should try for it. I really want to do it if you'll give me the chance."

"Mmmm, well quite a few students have signed up for the auditions so far, but we'll try to fit you in," Mr. Wingate replied.

"I was hoping to play that guy Sydney Carton," Jaris said. "That would be so awesome."

"Oh, is that right?" Mr. Wingate said with a sly smile. "You have no acting experience, but you've already believed yourself qualified for the leading role. Remarkable. Well, we'll see. I must say, Jaris Spain, you have attitude."

Jaris left the drama classroom without much hope. Mr. Wingate did not seem to like him. But he did give him a scene from the play featuring Sydney Carton to rehearse for the audition. When Jaris looked at it, he was amazed. It contained the powerful closing quote that Pop had remembered from his own school days.

"What if the incredible happened and I got the part," Jaris thought. "What if I got to wear all those cool costumes from the eighteenth century? What if I got to deliver those amazing lines? Maybe Sereeta would see me and change her mind about me. Maybe she'd stop comparing me to her dweeb cousin."

"Hey man," Trevor Jenkins said when he joined Jaris for lunch. Trevor just bought something to drink. His mom packed him something from home, usually tuna fish sandwiches. She thought that was brain food and her boys needed that. Jaris bought spaghetti at the school cafeteria. His mom didn't have time to pack lunches, not when she had to prepare lesson plans for her fourth-grade students.

"Hey Trevor," Jaris said. "I ran into B.J. the other day. Remember him?"

"Sure. He still a little guy?" Trevor asked.

"Yeah, but he's rolling in dough. It scared me, Trevor. He's not even a grown man yet, and he's in way over his head. I think he's dealing," Jaris said.

Trevor shrugged. "I was as bad as B.J. when I was younger. Difference is Mom wouldn't quit on me. She whupped me and she loved me too. I never doubted she would've died to save me. Even while I was cussing at her for whupping me, I knew she was on my side. B.J. never got that. His folks just gave up on him," he said. "I remember Mama caught me with a baggie one time, and she said the next time she's gonna kill me. I believed her too."

Jaris laughed. "No, she wouldn't of killed you," he said.

"I was afraid of her, man. I'm not fooling you. I was more afraid of Mama than I was afraid of the police or anybody else. We all were. Me and my brothers. She told us she'd rather have a dead son than a bad-to-the-bone son, so we just better never do a crime. Mama, she goes to church every Sunday, to the Holiness Awakening Church, and she sings up a storm, looks like an angel, but she is one tough mama," Trevor said.

"She's a good woman," Jaris asserted. "They don't come any better than her. She raised four good boys all by herself. She supported you without a man to help her. She's a hero, Trev. Look at your brothers—how good they're doing, and you too. You're making better grades than you ever did."

"I hear you man," Trevor said.

Jaris never knew the Jenkins family when there was a man around. By the time

Jaris and Trevor became friends, Mrs. Jenkins had been alone for ten years, working as a nurse's aide, doing two shifts sometimes, to keep her boys fed and clothed.

"You got any memories of your father, Trevor?" Jaris asked.

"Nah. He left when I was one or two years old. I've seen him, though. I've seen him coming out of places with his friends. He don't pay no attention to me. Funny, he looks like me. He don't pay no attention to my brothers either. Mama said he'd spend his pay on his own self, not us," Trevor said.

"You ever miss not having a dad around?" Jaris asked.

"No. You don't miss what you never had," Trevor said. "I'm glad he's not around. Who needs him?"

"Remember when we were all in junior high and Sereeta's parents got divorced, how hard she'd cry?" Jaris asked. "It really messed her up."

"Yeah. I guess maybe she had a good father. At least somebody who cared about her. She couldn't have felt so bad if he wasn't a good man," Trevor said. Then he made a face and said, "Man I hate these tuna fish sandwiches Mama makes. I'd like to toss them in the trash and buy a hot dog on a bun. Man, that'd be good."

"Why don't you do it?" Jaris asked.

"She'd know. Mama would know," Trevor said.

"How would she know? She's down working at the hospital," Jaris pointed out.

"I'm telling you, Jaris, she'd know. She knows everything," Trevor said.

"You know, Trev, sometimes I worry that my parents will break up. Mom hates it when Pop gets all moody and drinks before coming home. She always calls her mother and cries on her shoulder and then Grandma Jessie tells her she'd be better off without Pop. I worry that they'll split up," Jaris said.

"You got a good pop," Trevor said. "Mama took our old Ford in to Jackson's, and some other mechanic told her it needed a ton of work, and then your pop just tinkered a little bit and said we'd do fine. He's a good mechanic and he's honest. My mama trusts him. Everybody does. Old Jackson his boss sometimes gives him a hard time, but Jackson tells other people your pop is the best man he's ever had working for him."

"I wish my father was proud of what he did," Jaris complained, "but he's always putting himself down, calling himself a grease monkey. He wanted to go to college when he was young and now he's disappointed and he turns everything dark. He feels so hopeless and he sort of takes it out being sad and grumpy with Mom. I wish I could make him see that he's a winner."

CHAPTER FOUR

Grandma Jessie Clymer called Jaris on Tuesday evening. She usually didn't call him except on his birthday, which was a long way off. Grandma Jessie was Jaris's only grandparent. She was a widow. Both Pop's parents died young. So Grandma Jessie was the only grandparent and the only close relative from the older generation. Mom was an only child, and her mother lavished love and attention on her. She had near adoration for her beautiful, intelligent daughter: Monica Grace Clymer. The only time Monica stumbled in her mother's eyes was when she married Lorenzo Spain.

Jaris knew he should love his grandmother like Alonee loved hers and like Sereeta and Sami and Trevor loved theirs. But he didn't. He was polite to her, and, when she kissed him on the cheek, he didn't tell her that it made him sick.

Jaris not only did not love his grandmother, but sometimes he hated her.

"How are you, sweetheart?" Grandma Jessie asked him Tuesday evening. "Your mother tells me your last report card was wonderful. I'm not surprised. Your mother never earned less than an A in high school."

Jaris hated that Mom shared *everything* with her mother. When Jaris briefly dropped to a C in math last year, Grandma Jessie hired a tutor for him without even asking Jaris. Jaris refused to work with the tutor and brought his math grade up with the help of Pop, Alonee, and a study group at school. Grandma was very upset by Jaris's attitude. "I hope he isn't turning out like his father," she said.

"I'm doing good, Grandma," Jaris said to her inquiry on the phone.

"You must say you are doing 'well,'" she corrected him.

"Yeah, right," Jaris said.

"Sweetie," she said, "I do hope sloppy language isn't becoming a pattern for you. I worry about some of your friends. I understand you spend a lot of time with this Sami Archer girl. The poor child, in addition to having a weight problem she has an attitude and she's so loud. It's embarrassing. Once I came to Tubman as a member of the Friends of Tubman Society, and I noticed this terrible ruckus in the hall. Here she was, yelling and laughing, her and her wild friends."

Jaris gripped the phone so tightly that it made his fingers ache. "So Grandma, you called me about what?" He hoped she could detect the impatience in his voice.

"I wanted to take you to lunch on Saturday, Jaris," Grandma said.

"Uh, I work on Saturday," Jaris said.

"I'm sure you can get someone to fill in for you this once," Grandma Jessie said.

Mom came into the room then. She looked at Jaris with an intense stare. Jaris knew the look. It commanded him: "Do what Grandma wants. Don't disappoint Grandma, who loaned us the money to make the down payment on our home."

"I guess I could," Jaris said.

"Wonderful. I'll pick you up around eleven on Saturday, and we'll go to a nice restaurant. What kind of food do you like, Jaris? Chinese, Thai, French?"

"Fried chicken," Jaris said, "southern style."

"Oh my goodness!" Grandma exclaimed. "You're not destroying your arteries with that garbage, are you? I've told your mother a thousand times to serve healthy food. She knows that heart disease killed her father long before his time." Grandma sounded as if she were having a nervous breakdown.

"I was only kidding," Jaris answered quickly. "We eat really healthy foods—fish, salads, stuff like that. All low fat." It came out of cardboard boxes, frozen on dark plastic plates, but there *was* a lot of broccoli, rice, and salmon there.

"Well, good," Grandma went on. "So I'll choose a nice place. See you Saturday, sweetheart. Will you put your mother on the phone now?"

Jaris handed the phone to Mom. Then he went to his room. Even before he was completely out of the room, Mom lowered her voice and Jaris caught fragments of what she was saying. "He still does, yes, especially on the weekends. I've come to dread Friday nights. It makes me sick, but he doesn't think he has a problem."

Jaris turned around and went outside, his hands balled into fists. He was angry. He wanted to tell his grandmother how he resented her helping to turn Mom against Pop.

71

The door opened and Jaris's mother joined him. "Pretty moon tonight, huh sweetie? I wanted to be an astronomer when I was in my freshman year in college. I took several classes in astronomy. I'm one of the few people I know who can recognize a waning and waxing gibbous moon."

Jaris turned and glared at his mother. She was small and beautiful. She could have almost passed for a junior at Tubman if you didn't look too close and see the fine lines around her eyes. "Why do you have to tell Grandma *everything*?" Jaris growled, spitting out each word.

Mom's pleasant look vanished. She almost seemed frightened by the intensity of Jaris's voice. "Oh Jaris, don't be like that. It scares me when you're so angry. You remind me of your father and his dark moods," she said.

"You don't have to tell Grandma everything that happens in our family. We need to be loyal to each other, the four of us. A lot of the stuff should stay right here.

Nobody else needs to know," Jaris said bitterly. His mother went to church every Sunday. She led Bible study classes. She sang in the Praise choir. "You know the Bible so good, Mom. Doesn't it say there that a woman clings to her husband and him to her and not to their parents?"

"For heaven's sake, Jaris. She's my mother. I've always been close to her. We shared everything. We never had secrets from each other. Even when I was a teenager I shared with her," Mom said, taking a step toward Jaris, seeming to want to hug him and make everything better. But the anger in Jaris's face stopped her. "Sweetie, you and I are close, aren't we? I mean, you don't keep secrets from me, do you?"

"Yeah, I do," Jaris snapped. "All kids do. You did too but you won't admit it. But Mom, Grandma hates Pop and—"

"No, she doesn't hate your father. That's a terrible thing to say. Grandma is a good woman. She doesn't hate anybody. She's just a little disappointed that your father is so unhappy with his life that he has to drink too much," Mom explained.

"How does she know that he drinks too much?" Jaris demanded. "She's never around when he's drinking. But you tell her. You tell her every bad, shameful thing. It's like you got no respect for Pop. Maybe that's why he feels like trash. He's the husband and father around here, but you cut him down all the time with Grandma."

"Jaris!" Mom gasped, tears running down her face.

"Aw, for cryin' out loud, don't cry, Mom," Jaris groaned. "It's just that I wish you'd stop telling Grandma everything in our house. Like when I slipped in math, and she knew right away and hired some stupid tutor."

"Jaris, she did that out of love and concern for you," Mom said. "And he helped you bring up your grades didn't he?"

"No. Don't you remember? I wouldn't work with him. Pop and my friends from school helped me with math," Jaris said.

74

"All right," Mom agreed, "but your grandmother loves you, Jaris. She wants the best for you."

"Yeah? What's this stupid lunch on Saturday all about? I'm sure you know," Jaris said. "I'd rather spend Saturday digging weeds than be with her."

"What a cruel attitude, Jaris. My mother is a widow. Family is everything to her. Is it asking too much for you to spend a few hours with your only grandmother? She won't be around forever you know. She's almost seventy." Mom's voice was wavy with emotion.

There was a small stone bench in the backyard. Jaris sat down on it. He buried his face in his hands for a moment. "Okay, okay," he said. "But Mom, I gotta say this. I love my pop just like I love you and—"

"You think I don't love your father?" Mom cut in. "I love him too. I just don't love the way he is sometimes. He's a good mechanic. He makes good money. He has a family that loves him. Why does he have to dwell on the might-have-beens instead of all that he has."

Jaris got up and walked over to where his mother stood. He put his arms around her and hugged her. "I'm sorry, Mom. I know it's tough on you sometimes. It's just that I love both you guys—and you know, when Grandma Jessie is down on Pop it's like she's trying to burn our house down."

They went inside, and in about twenty minutes Pop came in. "I got hung up fixing a Honda with a blown radiator," he said. He didn't sound as if he'd been drinking, but he looked tired.

"Hey Pop, I know you're tired, but I wonder if you've got a coupla minutes to listen to me read something and tell me what you think?" Jaris said.

Pop stared silently at his son for a minute. Then he asked, "From that play you were talking about?"

"Yeah Pop. I'm doing an audition. Mr. Wingate gave me some stuff to rehearse.

I'd like you to listen and tell me if I seem to be getting the right tone," Jaris said.

The older man shook his head. "Boy, you need to be asking some of your buddies at school to listen to you. What do I know about acting?" he said.

"I know. I'll be asking them too. But Pop, you seemed to be really into that book. I just want you to tell me if I'm getting inside Sydney Carton's head in your opinion. Just give me a 'shoot from the hip' impression," Jaris said.

"Okay. Good enough," Pop said. "Let's go in the den." He seemed to walk a little straighter as they headed for the den. Pop really perked up. He reminded Jaris of the old Pop of several years ago, when he had some pride left.

"Okay," Jaris said and began to read from the script. His voice got stronger as he went along.

Pop shook his head. "No, not the right tone, Jaris. You got Carton sounding too triumphant. This guy has been beaten down for a lot of years. He spends most of his time in bars, drinking to escape the demons. He loved this girl, and she married somebody else. Now he's going to get his head chopped off in place of somebody else. This is a dude with a broken heart. You got to get the pathos, the sadness. . . ."

"Okay," Jaris said.

"See, Sydney Carton lost the girl he loved to this dude Charles Darnay. But he loves the girl so much that he is willing to die to save Darnay because he knows she loves him. Let me hear some grief. He knows he's doing a brave and noble thing, but he's coming from a deep dark place in his heart," Pop said.

Jaris did the reading again. He imagined how he felt when Sereeta ignored him even though he loved her. He recalled desperately trying to save her from being hurt by Marko Lane even though he had pretty much given up on ever having her affection. Jaris tried to imagine how far he

would go for Sereeta, and he put that
emotion into his reading.

"Much better!" Pop cried. "You almost
hit a home run, boy, but not quite. Keep
working on it. You sounded really good."

Jaris dreaded Grandma Jessie's little
red convertible pulling into the driveway
on Saturday. Grandma was a young sixty-
eight, fashionably dressed and well fixed.
She had made a lot of money in the real
estate boom and got out before the bubble
burst. She lived in a lovely condo with a
view of the bay.

"Hello Jaris," Grandma beamed as she
stepped from her car. She marched over
and gave Jaris a kiss. Then she drew back,
looking him up and down. "My, you're
more handsome every time I see you!"

"Thanks, Grandma. You look great."
She did too. She had beautiful skin, fine
bones, and silvery hair. "Well," she said,
"when you get to my age, nobody is looking
anymore, but I am determined to look as
well as I can."

Grandma drove to a quaint little seafood restaurant jutting out over the ocean. You could hear the waves crashing below. Jaris thought if he ever got the chance to take Sereeta to a terrific place, this would be it.

"I'll order for both of us," Grandma said. "I'm sure I'm more familiar with the menu here than you would be. Where you live, sweetheart, there are no places with cuisine like there is here."

"We live in a nice neighborhood, Grandma," Jaris said. "We got nice family restaurants."

Grandma Jessie smirked a little. An exotic shrimp entrée soon arrived with a lavish salad. Jaris had never seen such food. Grandma quickly launched into her agenda. "I'm sure you know, Jaris, that you children—you and Chelsea—are the world to me. I so want the best for you. You are my legacy."

"Yeah," Jaris said. He didn't want to be anybody's legacy. And the shrimp tasted funny. Jaris longed for the shrimp salad at Quick Eats in his neighborhood.

"I think you are capable of really going far, Jaris, but a fine plant flourishes only in the right environment. I am fearful that Tubman and your environs will hold you back . . ." Grandma had a sinister smile on her face. She was a nice looking older woman, but now she reminded Jaris of an evil witch stirring a cauldron, with smoke dancing before her face.

"Everything is fine where I am, Grandma," Jaris said.

"Did you know the dropout rate at Tubman is the highest in the city? You are surrounded by losers," Grandma said. "That has to affect your self-esteem."

"My self-esteem is good, Grandma," Jaris said. The salad tasted funny too. It was bathed in a strange sauce.

"The teachers at Tubman are third-rate. A few talented teachers are struggling against the odds, but most of them are inferior," Grandma's voice rushed on like a speeding train, unaffected by Jaris's comments.

"And then, sadly, there is your father, sweetheart. A dear man, I'm sure, but living with such negativism must be devastating to your own morale," Grandma said.

"Grandma," Jaris replied, "I'm auditioning for a play, and Pop is really helping me. The play is based on *A Tale of Two Cities,* and Pop really liked the book. He's giving me great pointers." Jaris felt his heart pounding. He felt as if he was in a battle of wits with a much more capable enemy.

"Jaris," Grandma said softly, "I have more money than I will ever need. I would like nothing more than to give you the chance to do your senior year at a marvelous private school in Santa Barbara."

"I don't want to change schools, Grandma," Jaris said—too loudly. "I like Tubman. I want to finish there with my friends."

"Dear, calm down. It's just an idea. You would live on the beautiful campus and associate with the finest young people in southern California. You would be insulated from all the bad influences in your life." Grandma Jessie paused to nibble delicately on her shrimp entrée. She looked up and smiled at Jaris. "Of course, I would cover all the expenses. Believe me, it would open up a whole new world for you."

"No," Jaris snapped. "Forget it. I mean, thanks for wanting to do something like that for me, but no way."

"Jaris, just think about it. Your mother is very open to the idea," Grandma said. Grandma's words came as a slap across Jaris's face. They—Mom and Grandma—plotted this.

CHAPTER FIVE

I get it," Jaris thought bitterly as Grandma Jessie drove him home. "They've been trying to find a way to ease Pop out. There's nobody on his side who can fight for him. Chelsea loves him, but she's too much of a kid yet to make a difference. Chelsea would cry a lot, like Sereeta did, but what could that accomplish?"

"Grandma," Jaris said as they neared home, "There's a guy I used to hang out with when I was a freshman. His folks pushed him really hard. They tried to make him into a different person than who he was. So he quit school and ran away. He disappeared into the streets. He lived in a ravine with other homeless kids for a while.

Now he's dealing drugs. His parents never see him anymore, and he's cool with that."

An angry look came to Grandma's face. "And what exactly is the point of that horrible little story, Jaris?" she asked.

"I'm just saying," Jaris explained, "that nobody's going to push me out of Tubman and being with my friends. The senior year, it's like what we all look forward to, doing it together. And another thing. Nobody is ever going to come between me and my pop. Nobody."

"Jaris, I am really saddened. I had no idea of how deeply your bad environment has already damaged your soul," Grandma commented.

"Yeah, well, I'm sorry," Jaris replied. "You got a good life, Grandma. You got lots of friends, and you can go travel and be happy in your life, but, you know, don't mess up my life, okay?"

After Grandma pulled into the Spain driveway, Jaris took off down the street. He texted Trevor to meet him at the Coffee

Camp. He figured Grandma Jessie and Mom would spend a long time talking. Pop was working late this Saturday on a special job, so he wouldn't be in the way. Chelsea was with her friends for a sleepover.

Grandma would tell Mom how rude and unappreciative Jaris was in the face of her generous offer. Grandma would roll her eyes and shake her head like she did when she was frustrated. She would probably say the evil genes of Lorenzo Spain were coming out in Jaris. Jaris didn't care. He was angry and resentful of what Grandma Jessie tried to do. Jaris didn't like how depressed and dark Pop got sometimes. It made Jaris depressed too. But Jaris loved his father. He wasn't willing to throw in the towel on Pop. Pop was still in the game. Maybe he wasn't hitting home runs, but he was still in the game.

"Hey Trevor, how you doing man?" Jaris greeted his friend with a grin.

"Yo dude, how you doing?" Trevor shot back.

"Oh, my Grandma wants me to ditch Tubman for my senior year and go to this ritzy school in Santa Barbara. You know, get me out of the 'hood. Away from all the bad influences. Mostly I figure she thinks it'd be good if I lived over at that school and Pop wasn't around me much anymore," Jaris said.

"No way!" Trevor exclaimed. "Man, we been living for being seniors at Tubman. That lady must be crazy. Nobody wants to switch schools for their senior year. Don't she remember nothin' about being a kid?"

"Well, I told her I wouldn't quit Tubman. No way. I came right out and told her I'd do something really wild and crazy if I got any pressure to quit Tubman," Jaris said. "You know, Trev, a really good thing is going on now with me and my pop. We're working together on my audition for the play. Pop loved that book, *A Tale of Two Cities*, when he was in school. He's giving me a lot of great ideas on how to get into the character of Sydney Carton."

"You said that Carton dude was a good man but sort of a loser who drowned his sorrows in the bottle. Maybe your pop sees a little of himself in Carton," Trevor suggested.

"Maybe," Jaris said. "I can see a difference in Pop since he's been helping me. The man has pride. Been kind of ignored for a long time. You know, Trev, I didn't even think of going for the part until Alonee kept nagging me. Now I'm glad I did. Wouldn't it be amazing if I got to play Sydney Carton and Sereeta would see me in a whole new way. But I'm not getting my hopes up too high. I mean, I don't think that dude Wingate has much use for me."

Jaris got home in the early evening. Grandma Jessie was long gone. Jaris steeled himself for a scolding from Mom. Grandma probably dissed him good.

"Hi Mom," Jaris said when he came in. His strategy was to pretend that nothing had happened. But to his surprise Mom seemed in a good mood. She was all dressed up in a pretty pale blue suit, and her briefcase was on the kitchen table. "Sweetie, my principal is coming over this evening. There's that new language arts program for third and fourth grades, and he wants me to give him my input. We have to get all the snags out before we begin using it. We'll probably go down to the coffee shop and find a quiet booth where we can talk. Chelsea has two girls coming over, and you know what that will sound like!" Mom smiled.

"Okay," Jaris said. "Pop's not home yet, huh?"

"No, not yet. I guess they're really busy at the garage. People who used to buy cars every few years are getting the old ones fixed up instead," Mom explained, looking at her watch.

"Oh," Mom said suddenly, "there he is now!"

Jaris misunderstood his mother. He thought she meant Pop had come home.

But there was a strange car in the driveway: a silver Honda.

"Hi Greg," Mom said, opening the front door as he approached. "Greg, this is my son, Jaris. He's a junior at Tubman, a very good student I'm proud to say."

The principal, Greg Maynard, was young. He looked about Mom's age. He had a buzz haircut and he was very fit. He reminded Jaris of a basketball coach they once had at Tubman. He was handsome with cocoa-colored skin and bright eyes. "Hello Jaris. I must say I wouldn't expect my best teacher's son to be anything but a good student."

Jaris disliked the man instantly. He was too glib, too phony. He sounded like he should be selling sleazy securities to retired people instead of teaching. Jaris didn't like the way Maynard smiled at Mom either. Jaris knew that making snap judgments was not wise, but Maynard just did not seem like the real deal.

Chelsea's two giggling girlfriends arrived as Mom and Maynard were leaving. When the silver Honda pulled away, one of the girls, Jackina, sighed, "Oooooo, isn't he cute? How come none of the teachers at our school look like that?"

"All our teachers are so old," Chelsea said.

The other friend of Chelsea's said, "He looks just like that guy who won the Oscar, that slick dude who just got a divorce from his first wife."

Jaris had a bad feeling about the whole thing. Greg Maynard seemed to like Mom, and she seemed to like him. Maynard was attractive, charming, and funny. They had a lot in common. Maynard seemed like the type of guy Grandma Jessie wished Mom had married in the first place.

Before Chelsea joined her friends in her bedroom, she stopped alongside Jaris and said, "His daughter goes to my school. I've seen him picking her up."

"Whose daughter?" Jaris asked.

"Mr. Maynard's," Chelsea replied. "She's in the seventh grade. She's real pretty but she's kind of stuck up."

Jaris smiled. Well, at least the guy was married. So he wouldn't be getting ideas about Mom. But then Chelsea went on, "She lives with her mother most of the time but he gets her on Friday."

"Oh . . . then they're divorced," Jaris said, his heart sinking.

"Yeah, for a long time. He lives in a fancy condo near downtown. Elise told me about the marble in the bathroom and stuff, and she goes there to be with her dad because of the amazing spa," Chelsea said.

Chelsea then hurried off to be with her friends.

Jaris tried to put the whole issue out of his mind. Mom was a married woman. She loved Dad. Didn't she say that? Mom would never get mixed up with another guy. It was crazy. But Jaris had let his imagination run away with him. He trembled a little. He was getting more and more like Pop, seeing demons where none existed.

At school on Monday, Jaris overheard a good-looking guy in his history class talking about the play. DeWayne Pike said he was trying out for the part of Sydney Carton. "That's the plum part," DeWayne said, "and I think I have a shot at it. I have lots of experience. I was in the *Nutcracker* when I was just a kid, and I've done a couple plays here at Tubman, one in ninth grade and two when I was a sophomore. I know my way around a stage."

Sereeta was looking at DeWayne as he spoke. It looked like admiration in her face. "I saw you in *Fiddler on the Roof*, and you were so good," she oozed.

Jaris felt sick. Pike was handsome, and he had acting experience. Why shouldn't Wingate pick him? Alonee leaned over and whispered to Jaris, "Your voice is better than his. And you've got the heart to play Sydney Carton."

"Thanks for the vote of confidence," Jaris said. But he figured Alonee was just being nice. "But I think he's got it. I know when I'm beat."

After a discussion of the Great American Depression, Ms. McDowell began shooting questions out at her students. "So how did this great economic crisis change the way the U.S. government dealt with its citizens?"

"Uh," Derrick Shaw waved his hand in the air, "it proved how stupid the government was."

Ms. McDowell scowled. She turned to DeWayne, "Yes?"

"Well, it kind of made the government get into stuff they weren't into before," he said.

"You are on the right track, DeWayne," Ms. McDowell said. Her hopeful gaze wandered over the room in search of a better answer. Jaris remembered his father telling him about his own grandfather during the Depression. Pop's grandparents were starving. Sometimes they would go into restaurants, order a bowl of hot water, and mix catsup with it to make soup. It was all they had. Then President Franklin D.

Roosevelt came along to set up programs to give work to the unemployed. Jaris raised his hand. "Well, before the Depression the government thought all they had to do was defend the people against enemies in war and stuff, but when the Depression hit, President Roosevelt said the government had to make sure people didn't starve or go homeless. That was the job of government too. Ever since then, when the economy is bad, the government steps up to help the people, like with unemployment insurance."

"Excellent, Jaris. Exactly right. You must have read Chapter 12 quite thoroughly," Ms. McDowell said.

"I did, yeah, but my father told me a lot of stuff about his grandparents in the Depression," Jaris said. He noticed Sereeta was smiling at him. Sereeta admired brains. She liked cute boys, but she preferred brains.

After class, Sereeta caught up to Jaris. "Alonee told me you're trying out for the play too, Jaris," she said. "You want to play Sydney Carton."

Jaris did what he usually did when Sereeta was in front of him. He got a stupid attack. "Well, yeah. I mean, I never acted, and I probably don't have a chance or anything, but who knows?" he sputtered.

"Have you read *A Tale of Two Cities*, Jaris?" Sereeta asked.

"Sort of. I didn't read the whole thing, but I read a lot of pages, especially where Carton comes in. Mr. Wingate gave me the play outline to rehearse," Jaris said.

"Sydney Carton is the hero," Sereeta told him, "but Charles Darnay is the other major male role. In the book, both men look alike, not exactly alike but close. You know what's spooky, Jaris? You and DeWayne sort of look alike. He's heavier than you and you're a little darker, but you're both handsome."

Jaris felt numb. He couldn't believe what Sereeta had just said: "*But you're both handsome .*"

For at least a few seconds, Jaris was dancing on air currents. It might have appeared that his feet were on the ground, but that simply was not the truth.

Finally Jaris found his voice and said, "Why don't you try out for the play too, Sereeta? It'd be fun if we'd be in the play together."

Sereeta laughed. "Well, there's one nice role for a girl, Lucie Manette. She's Darnay's wife, but Carton loves her too. All the other female roles are really strange," she said.

At that moment, Sami Archer joined them. "I want to be Miss Pross. She ends up beating the stuffin' out of that old broad— Madame DeFarge—that old she devil. Says in the book that Miss Pross is one tough chick. That would be cool to play her. I'd never want to be that little twit, Lucie. All that girl does is faint or cry. I mean, like who needs a chick like that? Got to keep picking her up off the floor."

Marko Lane stood at the edge of the group talking about the play. He listened for a moment, then he said, "This Miss Pross you want to play, Sami—is she a dog too?" A cruel sneer turned his lips. He was one of the students bullying Sami since middle school. Back then Sami was more vulnerable. Since then, she developed a good self-image and now was stronger. "You're so mean and stupid, Marko Lane, only part you could play would be a snake," she said.

"Well," Marko said, "if they pick you to play this Miss Pross, she must be one ugly babe."

Jaris was furious at Marko for his cruelty, but, before he could say anything, Sereeta stepped forward. "Marko," she said, "you are making such a pathetic fool of yourself. I mean, you need to get help for all that hostility."

Marko looked stunned. For a girl, especially one as pretty as Sereeta, to cut him down like that shocked him. He was one of the handsomest boys at Tubman. He could date pretty much whom he wanted. "Hey, excuse me," Marko finally retorted, "I didn't think you were that tight with a chick from Grant Avenue, Sereeta. I mean, you're setting your sights pretty low to hang in with the graffiti gangbangers from Grant Avenue."

"Kids from Grant are as good as you are, Marko Lane, and lots better too," Sami yelled, finding her attitude. "Don't matter the street you live on. Matters what's in your heart and soul, and you ain't got much in either place."

A crowd was gathering to watch the fireworks. Sami was well liked by most of the students. They cheered her sassy talk. Marko was humiliated. He skulked off to the laughter of the small crowd.

When Jaris got home from school, he seriously resolved to read as much of *A Tale of Two Cities* as he could. He wanted to learn as much as he could about the story. But, as he got into the book, he heard yelling coming from the kitchen. It was unusual to hear Mom yelling but she was yelling now.

"You could at least take off those filthy clothes and shower. You could at least do that. You could have that much respect for your wife and children!" Mom was shouting.

Ice water went down Jaris's spine.

Jaris stayed in his room. He didn't want to shame Pop by going out there.

"The dirt on me won't wash off with soap and water," Pop said. "It's gotten to my soul."

"Oh, for heaven's sakes, Lorenzo, don't be so dramatic. How do you think it made me feel when Mrs. Harvey came over to return my blender, and she could smell you the minute she came to the door? How do you think it made me feel? You don't even shave half the time anymore!" Mom shouted.

Jaris buried his face in his hands. He felt totally helpless. He understood how Mom felt. There were times she didn't even want Pop to come to church with her, even on those rare occasions when he wanted to come, because he hadn't showered. She was ashamed of the fact that he did not take care of himself like he used to. Mom was always clean and smart looking. Most of their friends—the couples they had dinner with—were the same. Jaris knew his father stood out in a bad way.

But he was Pop and Jaris loved him.

A door slammed. The yelling stopped.

Chelsea crept into Jaris's room, her eyes wide. She had such a cheerful spirit that most of the time problems bounced off her, but now she looked as if she had been crying. "Oh Jaris, poor Pop had a terrible day at the garage. They screwed up some guy's engine, and Jackson blamed Pop. Then they found out some other guy messed up, but Pop was so ticked off by then, he went to a bar and. . . ." Chelsea shook her head. "Then this creepy Mrs. Harvey comes in and makes this gross face, and Mom just exploded. You know how proud Mom is. And you know Mrs. Harvey is going to spread it all over the neighborhood, even at church. The women are going to gossip. 'Poor Mrs. Spain, what a gross husband she has.' "

"Man," Jaris said. "I'd like to find a cave and crawl in it."

When Jaris finally went out to the living room, Mom was on the computer. The shower was running. Pop was finally cleaning up, but too late. Mom looked up from the computer and said, "Jaris, you and Chelsea get something from the freezer—stick it in the microwave. There's a nice salmon and vegetables, or some egg rolls. I'm really hammered for time. I've got to finish this work for school. Greg . . . uh, Mr. Maynard, expects my evaluation in the morning for a staff meeting."

"Sure Mom," Jaris replied, "we'll be fine."

Jaris and Chelsea silently fixed dinner and ate it, then hurried back to their rooms.

Jaris opened *A Tale of Two Cities* and started reading. Some of it was tough going. Turned out Sydney Carton was an attorney. Smart, Jaris figured. You had to be smart to be an attorney. But wait—Jaris read more intently.

"Sydney Carton, idlest and most unpromising of men."

The story continued. Carton, in mussed-up clothing, was seen going home unsteadily to the place where he lived, "like a dissipated cat." Jaris looked up the word *dissipated* in the dictionary. "Showing physical effects of a dissolute life." He was wasted by drink. He was a sad and bitter man.

CHAPTER SIX

The explosion of the night before at the Spain house had left some damage, as explosions do. Jaris and his sister sat at the breakfast table eating their oatmeal, sliced cantaloupe, and scrambled eggs. Mom nibbled on everything but didn't eat much of anything. She put out Pop's breakfast, but when he appeared in the doorway he said, "I'll grab something later at the diner." And then he left. He didn't look at anybody. In seconds the green pickup roared to life, and he was gone.

"Well," Mom said. Just that. "Well." She dumped Pop's breakfast in the garbage, except for the chunks of cut cantaloupe, which she put in the refrigerator. Then

Mom explained, "I hurt his feelings last night. But for crying out loud, doesn't a man owe his family common hygiene? Cleanliness is next to godliness. Isn't that the time-honored tradition?" Mom seemed to be trying to justify the harshness of her treatment of Pop last night. Then she started feeling sorry for herself.

"It will be the talk of the town," she said ruefully. "Mrs. Harvey will see to that. Her children go to my school. She's active in PTA." Mom changed her voice to mimic Mrs. Harvey's voice. "Poor Monica Spain. Have you seen her husband lately? Looks like one of those homeless men begging for food. Smells like one too. You can smell him a mile off. It is so tragic."

Chelsea broke into her mother's words. "Pop just had a bad day. He's not like that all the time. That old Mrs. Harvey is such a big gossip. A lot of people hate her. Who cares what she says?"

"I care," Mom snapped. "Don't you think I want to be proud of your father?

He's a fine looking man. I'd be so proud of him when he'd take me out on dates when we were young." She had a sad, wistful look on her face.

"Mom," Jaris said, "you can be proud of Pop. Everybody respects him as a good mechanic and an honest man. That's what's important."

Mom was teary-eyed when Jaris finished. "I know, I know," she moaned.

Jaris grabbed his backpack, then headed for school. He was glad his mother was feeling a little guilty over some of the things she said. That was a good sign. Halfway to Tubman, Jaris ran into Alonee. She usually left earlier, but this morning they got to walk to school together. "You read much of *A Tale of Two Cities*, Jaris?" she asked.

"Yeah. I was surprised at this guy Carton. I thought he was a big shot lawyer, but he was like a street bum a lot of the time. He'd stagger home from the bars looking all messed up. The guy had problems," Jaris said.

"I guess we all do," Alonee said.

Jaris smiled at Alonee. "Always seems to me like you got it pretty much together, girl," he said.

Alonee shrugged. "You might be surprised. Some of us are just better at hiding our feelings than others. Don't know if that's good or bad. Let too much hang out, and nobody wants to be around you. But if you keep too much in, then nobody even knows you," she said, suddenly laughing. "Am I getting too mysterious for you, Jaris?"

Jaris always liked Alonee. They knew each other all their lives. She was sweet and dependable Alonee. She always had your back in tough situations. "You got deep, dark secrets, Alonee?" Jaris asked her.

"We all do—everybody," she said.

"If you're so good at acting like somebody you're not, then why don't you try out for the play too, Alonee?" Jaris asked.

"No. Acting isn't for me," Alonee answered. "I wouldn't want to get up in front of all those people and act. Besides, I have this little voice. Nobody could hear me. There's nothing worse than not being able to hear the lines."

"You're such a weirdo, Alonee," Jaris commented. "You put yourself down. The truth is you have a nice voice. And you could do anything you tried to do."

"Thank you, sir," Alonee said, "for the compliment."

As Tubman High School loomed, Jaris was already anticipating seeing Sereeta in American History I. It was the highlight of his day. He always wondered what she'd be wearing. She favored pullover sweaters in bright colors. They really brought out her figure.

Sereeta was wearing tight-fitting jeans and a red pullover. She smiled at Jaris before she sat down.

Ms. McDowell, the teacher, was a young, slim black woman with only a few years' experience, but she ran a tight ship. She could bully a six-foot-three football player into submission with her icy stare.

Jaris figured she was a born teacher. Jaris figured there were people destined to do certain jobs, and they wouldn't excel as much anywhere else.

A feeling of sadness swept over Jaris. Pop was such a good mechanic he could earn top money at any garage. Even Jackson was always giving him bonuses to keep him there. Pop could take anything apart and put it back together, but he found no joy in that. So what was the good of a gift you didn't want? Pop dreamed of a college education and a career in science. He imagined himself coming up with dramatic new products. When it didn't happen, he couldn't find satisfaction in the skills he had.

Jaris found it hard to concentrate in history with Sereeta sitting ahead of him. He stared at the beautiful contours of her face. When she turned a little, Jaris caught sight of her delicate ear, like a seashell tucked among her black curls. He admired the way her shoulders curved. She was so

109

perfect. He began fantasizing about the play, about him playing Sydney Carton and her playing Lucie. They had known each other for years, but this would be the first time they worked together on a project. Jaris imagined her looking at him and crying, "Oh Jaris, I never knew you could be this much fun!"

Jaris was completely lost in his dreams when Ms. McDowell interrupted them: "So, Jaris, was President Roosevelt right in trying to pack the Supreme Court with more justices?" Shocked out of his reverie, Jaris stared stupidly at the teacher. Still looking at Jaris, she asked, "Can you tell me *why* the president tried to do this?"

Sereeta raised her hand. "The Supreme Court was overturning a lot of Roosevelt's programs," Sereeta answered. "The justices were older men, and they didn't agree with the new ideas of the government trying to fix the Depression problems."

"Exactly," Ms. McDowell said in a pleased voice. "Roosevelt wanted to appoint younger members more attuned to his radical ideas."

Derrick Shaw had a question. When he raised his hand, Ms. McDowell looked pained.

"Teacher, how many people are on the Supreme Court? Is it like the Senate—one for each state?"

Muffled laughter rumbled through the classroom. If such a question had been posed in poor Mr. Pippin's class, there would have been a riot of amusement. But Ms. McDowell glared at the titterers and said to Derrick, "There are nine."

"Wow," Derrick said, "nine for each state?"

"No Derrick, nine total," Ms. McDowell stated grimly. "As for the Senate, there are *two* members for each state."

Jaris felt sorry for Derrick. He was dumb. That was all there was to it. You couldn't sugarcoat it. Jaris was grateful that he wasn't as dumb as Derrick, but he knew he wasn't as smart as Sereeta either.

He wondered if she'd ever want to be the girlfriend of a boy not as smart as she was. That was the question even if he did get to play Sydney Carton—and he doubted he would.

Jaris wondered if Mom was smarter than Pop. Mom graduated from college magna cum laude, with high honors. Pop made good grades in high school, but he probably wouldn't have aced college like Mom did. Maybe Mom sort of looked down on Pop from the beginning because she knew she was smarter. Maybe Pop sensed that, and that was why he was so bitter.

"I'm not dumb like Derrick," Jaris told himself. "I got an A average right now. Sure I had to work my tail off for it, but I got it. And I *knew* the answer to Ms. McDowell's Supreme Court question too. I just couldn't get it out fast enough."

After class, the students filed out of history. Marko Lane and a couple of his friends were lurking. Jaris could see from the looks on their faces that they were spoiling for a fight. As Sereeta went by them, Marko moved in. He wanted to get even with her for humiliating him the other day. "Hey Sereeta," Marko yelled, "I got it figured out why you're so buddy-buddy with Sami. You're getting fat too. You better quit wearing those size two jeans girl."

Sereeta hadn't put on an extra pound all year, but Marko's slur hurt her. At first she ignored Marko, but then he yelled, "Been scarfin' down too many burritos, fat girl? You better lay off those supersized burgers."

"Shut up, freak," Jaris shouted, enraged that Marko would attack Sereeta like this. "Shut your dirty mouth or I'll shut it for you."

"Listen to the skinny little weakling bellow," Marko laughed. "I could have you for lunch, fool."

Mr. Pippin happened to be walking by. He looked horrified. He sensed that a fight was about to break out and, as a faculty member, he would be expected to intervene. Mr. Pippin was slightly built and in his early sixties. All he lived for was escaping the classroom and spending the rest of his life in some peaceful place, living on his pension. Now Mr. Pippin stared at Marko and his burly friends in terror. He imagined himself pounded to the pavement by these brutes, who now advanced toward Jaris and two other boys. Mr. Pippin could already feel the sickening sensation of breaking ribs or a shattered hip. But he couldn't run. He was trapped with the obligation to somehow stop the fight. Fate had dealt him one last, perhaps fatal, blow.

Suddenly a boy screamed, "Cops! Here come the cops!" It was Derrick Shaw sounding the alarm. Marko Lane was about to plant a beefy fist into the middle of Jaris's face when Shaw's warning stopped him cold. Marko spun around and fled, his friends behind him. None of them wanted to be busted and perhaps expelled from Tubman.

Jaris looked around. He didn't see any police. And he wondered what the police would be doing at the school anyway. Then he glanced at Derrick, who was grinning.

"I thought I better do something," Derrick said. "I thought saying the cops were coming would stop it."

Mr. Pippin turned to Derrick, a look of abject gratitude on his face. "What a splendid show of good judgment, young man. You averted a terrible fight in which our students could have been injured." What he actually was saying to Derrick was "Thank you for saving *me* from disaster."

"That was pretty smart, Derrick," Jaris said.

"Yeah, I thought they'd scatter like pigeons if the cops were coming. They did too, huh? I hate fights," Derrick replied.

Jaris clapped the other boy on the back. "We all owe you one, man," he said.

Sereeta walked with Jaris to her next class. She had biology and Jaris had science. Sereeta's biology class was the hardest in the science department. Jaris had opted for basic science, a much easier course. "Marko is really a creep," Sereeta said.

"I liked him for a while. He's a good athlete and he can be nice. But he's a creep."

Sereeta put her hand on Jaris's arm. "But Jaris," she insisted, "promise me you won't take his bait again. I know he was trying to hurt me, but I'm a big girl. I think it's sweet that you want to be a knight in shining armor, but let's just ignore Marko. It'd be terrible if he got you in trouble for fighting. You know school policy. Doesn't matter who starts a fight. Fighting gets a suspension or maybe worse. Promise me, okay? I'd never forgive myself if you got in trouble trying to defend me."

Jaris was deeply touched. Sereeta sounded so sincere, like she really cared what happened to Jaris. That meant she liked him at least a little bit, didn't it?

Later, in science, Mr. Buckingham was discussing endangered species. "We all know the usual suspects, the gray whales, the whooping cranes. But for your reports I want you to dig out the more unusual endangered species. Little known creatures who still form a vital part of earth's ecosystem."

Mr. Buckingham was a tall, dark-skinned man with silvery hair. He had a dignity about him that commanded attention. His voice rolled like thunder. He traced his own ancestry to Askia the Great, who built the Songhay Empire in the Sudan in the fifteenth century.

"People, the mass extinction of species going on right now is called the Holocene event. Tens of thousands of species may be lost every year," Mr. Buckingham intoned.

The students went to the charts and photographs around the room to choose a subject. Jaris signed up for the Madagascar fish eagle. Alonee chose the Honduran emerald hummingbird. Trevor finally chose the hermit ibis.

Jaris had to work two shifts at the Chicken Shack to make up for taking time off to have lunch with Grandma Jessie last Saturday. Instead of getting home around nine, he was walking down Grant Street after midnight. When a car turned a corner and its headlights illuminated a block wall, Jaris saw the new graffiti. Lurid red and blue letters leaped out at him. "Wow," Jaris muttered to himself, "this is pretty close to our neighborhood. They usually don't happen this far north."

A boy jumped from the shadows. "You got a problem, man?" he demanded. Jaris had been staring at the new tagging. Now he turned abruptly. The first boy was joined by two others. Jaris recognized one of them as a Tubman dropout from last year. He usually sat in the back of his classes, dressed in oversized denims and red sneakers. He was good at baseball too. He was on the Tubman Tigers baseball team until he was busted for drugs and expelled from the school.

With the three boys in a semicircle around him, Jaris felt threatened. From out of the past, Shane "Sparky" Burgess's name came to him. He was the kid with the red sneakers. "Hey, Sparky, I remember that game against the Wilson Wolverines. You had the most amazing fastball I ever saw. You were electric. You gave us the game."

Shane Burgess stood there with a strange expression on his face. For a few seconds the hostility faded, and there was the trace of a smile. "Dog," he said, "*you remember me?*"

"Sure," Jaris said. He looked at the others then. "I got no bone to pick with you guys. I'm just going home from work."

Jaris walked on. He wasn't sure he was out of the woods yet, but he didn't turn back to see if the guys were still there. He just kept walking and praying a little. And when he turned off Grant, he did look back and nobody was there.

Jaris breathed a sigh of relief.

Jaris racked his brain trying to remember more about Shane Burgess. He always seemed like an outsider. Most of the students at Tubman were from Jaris's neighborhood, kids he'd grown up with. But when they start building the apartments on Grant Avenue, there was an influx of new people. Burgess was one of them. Most of those kids were from single-family homes led by a mother. Because of them, the dropout rate at Tubman shot up.

The next day after school, Jaris texted Trevor to see if he remembered Shane Burgess. All he remembered was the red shoes. Jaris called Sami. "Yeah, I remember that dude. He was an odd duck. Never said nothing to nobody, but the baseball made him come alive. Seen him the last time after he got suspended . . . looked like he was crying. He was tossing a baseball back and forth in his hands," Sami said. "I figured baseball was gonna be his ticket outta whatever dark hole he was caught up in, but it didn't get to happen."

"I ran into him and some other tough-looking guys tagging a wall when I was coming home last night from the Chicken Shack," Jaris said.

"Were they tagging closer to our neighborhood, Jare?" Sami asked.

"Afraid so," Jaris said.

"Whoa! Hey Jaris, if you still got your curiosity about Shane Burgess going, you ask Alonee Lennox. She took a real interest in him," Sami remembered.

Jaris called Alonee. It was easy for him to see Alonee reaching out to some lost kid like Shane. That was her.

"Yeah, I remember Sparky," Alonee said. "You see him?"

"Yeah, him and two other gangbangers were tagging a wall on Grant when I was coming home from work," Jaris said.

"Awww, I was hoping he'd found a good place. But he had his demons. You know, Ms. McDowell tried to help him too. It was her first year here at Tubman, and I'd see her giving him a lift home when it was raining," Alonee said.

"Yeah? I wouldn't imagine her doing something like that. I mean she's a great teacher but she's . . ." Jaris couldn't think of the exact word.

"Cold," Alonee finished his sentence. "She bonded with Shane. I never could understand it. People are funny. They say we don't even know ourselves, and we sure don't know what's going on in other peoples' heads."

Jaris hung up then and tried to study for a big test coming up in Mr. Pippin's class. They had read what seemed like hundreds of poems from the nineteenth century. Jaris was afraid that, when the test was in front of him, all the names and titles would swim together and he'd flunk.

CHAPTER SEVEN

Jaris reread the poems they had studied in Mr. Pippin's class until he was so tired his eyes wouldn't stay open. He went to bed and fell asleep immediately.

Then, around midnight, he heard voices coming through his wall from his parents' bedroom. They were angry voices and Jaris stiffened.

"Another meeting with your principal?" Pop asked. "Why don't you move over there. You're never home nights anymore."

"I told you, Lorenzo, there's a new language arts program that is very important. I'm helping Mr. Maynard make the transition. The school board expects all third and fourth grades to show results in the next testing period," Mom explained in her patient but scolding voice. Jaris noticed that, more and more, Mom was using the same voice to talk to Pop as she did with her children.

"Maynard seems like a jerk," Pop snapped. "I've seen his kind before. He's one of those oily guys, all charm and nothing to back it up. Book smart but without good sense. Seems to me if he's a big shot principal, he oughtn't be trying to pick the brains of a poor little fourth-grade teacher like you."

Jaris winced. He knew where Pop was coming from. Maybe Greg Maynard was enjoying Monica Spain's company more than he was needing her advice. Maybe all those language arts meetings had more to do with Mom's being beautiful and delightful than her being an educational expert. But Mom was sure to be insulted by Pop's comment. "Maybe Mr. Maynard sees qualities in me you don't, Lorenzo. I mean, I'm not just a 'little fourth-grade teacher.' I am a well respected member of the team at that school, and Mr. Maynard values my input very much," Mom said in a hurt voice.

"You sure this dude isn't getting to like your company too much, Monie? I'm hearing he hasn't got any lady of his own and maybe he's lonely. Maybe . . ." Pop's voice was harsh and bitter.

"Lorenzo, I am so hurt and offended that you would suggest such a thing," Mom protested, her voice rising.

"You can act high and mighty, girl," Pop said, "but I know you haven't been satisfied with me for a long time now. *Don't you think I know*? Here comes this fine dude in good threads, and he smells of pricey cologne, and maybe being with him is way better than being with your man."

"I'm not going to listen to anymore of this garbage," Mom yelled. "Yeah, I'm sick and tired of how you've been acting, buddy, but it has nothing to do with Mr. Maynard." Mom didn't sound like herself now. She sounded tough and hard. "You better wise up, Lorenzo Spain. You been sinking into this pity party for too freakin' long. You been pulling me down and pulling the kids down. So knock if off, buddy. You got a good job, and a lotta men would get on their knees and thank the Almighty for the kind of money you make. Lot of good men are unemployed, working a few days a week if they're lucky. You got your health, a good job, and a family that cares about you. So just get some sense in that thick head of yours before it's too late for all of us!"

Jaris hated hearing his parents fight, but he was glad Mom had the courage to lay it on the line like that. Pop needed to hear what she was saying.

There was silence from his parents' room now, but Jaris couldn't go back to sleep. He started thinking about the test tomorrow, about the play, about Sereeta, about the kind of science report he could do on the impending fate of the Madagascar fish eagle. He thought about those three boys he met at the wall, and he worried that the gang influence was getting closer. But mostly he worried about his parents. Had this latest fight succeeded in clearing the air and making things better? Or had it only deepened the rift between his parents?

In the morning, Jaris was tired. He'd just about gotten to sleep when the alarm rang, telling him the new day had arrived, the day of Mr. Pippin's test. Jaris was barely hanging onto an A minus in English. As bad a teacher as Mr. Pippin was, he was a tough grader. If Jaris blew this test, he could lose his overall A average for his junior year.

Jaris crawled out of bed feeling like a zombie. He had studied the poems and sort of understood their meanings, but you never knew what Pippin would pull.

Breakfast time was strained. Mom put out the pancakes she had unfrozen in the microwave. She put out warm muffins and cantaloupe slices. Pop didn't say anything, but he stayed for breakfast. Jaris searched his mind for some safe topic of conversation to break the icy atmosphere.

"We got a test in English today," Jaris finally said. "Lot of dumb poetry. Mr. Pippin loves these really confusing poems with all sorts of hidden meanings."

Before Pop could comment, Mom cut in sharply. "Don't call it dumb poetry, Jaris. You need to develop an appreciation for it."

Chelsea was in a good mood. She had slept soundly last night, being far enough away from her parents' bedroom to miss the quarrel. "I like limericks. They are so fun.

'There once was a fellow named Drummy,

'He got sick and died,

'and everyone cried,

'Now they turned him into a mummy.'"

"Oh Chelsea!" Mom scolded. But her lips betrayed her. She was smiling.

Pop cleared his throat. He was chuckling.

Jaris winked at Chelsea.

"How are the auditions for the play

coming, Jaris?" Pop asked, now that the ice was broken.

"The audition isn't for another couple weeks," Jaris said. "I'm hoping Sereeta gets in the play too. It'd be fun for the both of us to work together."

Pop smiled. "Lucie is a weak character," he stated. "When it came to writing about women, Dickens was old school. The nice ones like Lucie were frail. The only strong women in *A Tale of Two Cities* are the villainess Madame DeFarge and that Miss Pross, who does her in. I would call Miss Pross the heroine of the story. Poor Lucie is a wimp. Miss Pross, now she was a holy terror."

Mom glared at Pop. She seemed to think he was comparing her to Miss Pross, that she was strong and controlling. But before Mom could say anything, Pop got up noisily, grating his chair back. "Well, nothing gets a man off on the right foot more than a hearty breakfast. Thank you Miss Butterfinger for the hot pancakes, and thank you Aunt Elsie for the muffins. You girls are doing just fine." Pop smiled at the boxes of pancakes and frozen muffins.

Mom glared at Pop again. "I'm sorry I can't make things from scratch. I happen to be a working woman."

"I make enough money for this family to live on, Monie. I can pay all the bills and have some left over if you want to spend more time in the kitchen," Pop said.

"I trained for five years to be an educator, and I'm not wasting all those years making muffins from scratch!" Mom snorted.

"Heaven forbid," Pop said in an amiable voice. He looked at Jaris and Chelsea and whispered, "Way to go, Madame DeFarge."

Jaris suppressed a smile. He didn't want to annoy Mom anymore than she was already irritated. When Pop was out the door and off in his green pickup, Mom turned to her children and said, "He doesn't miss a chance to give me a dig."

"He was just joking, Mom," Jaris said. Half to get Mom's mind off Pop, Jaris asked, "You know my history teacher, Ms. McDowell, don't you?"

"Yes. I've met her on open house nights. She seems excellent," Mom responded.

"Yeah, she's great. She usually doesn't get too close to students, but she got close to a guy who's dropped out of Tubman. Shane Burgess. He was a pretty good baseball player. Then he got in trouble, and he was kicked out of Tubman. I ran into him the other night. He and some guys were tagging a wall."

Mom stood there for a moment, as if she was trying to decide what to say. Then Jaris could tell she was about to say something important: "This is in the strictest confidence, Jaris. Don't share it with anybody. When Ms. McDowell came to Tubman she was a real success story. She's from a very dysfunctional family. Shane is her half brother. She tried very hard to help him."

"Oh," Jaris assured her. "I won't say a word about it, Mom, I swear." Jaris would not have broken Mom's confidence even if he did not care for Ms. McDowell. But he really respected Ms. McDowell, and he wouldn't do anything that put her in a bad light. She was Jaris's favorite teacher at Tubman.

Later at school, Jaris walked into the English classroom and settled into his chair. Mr. Pippin began passing out the tests immediately. When Jaris read the first few questions, he felt as if ice water had been dumped on his head. It seemed as if every single poem they read was on the test. There were questions about symbolism and deep meanings.

Jaris felt he did pretty well on the true/false and multiple-choice questions. He could match most of the poets with their poems. But the essay question was his undoing. He was supposed to choose one of the major poets they had studied and write at length about his works. Jaris did not completely understand any of the poets, but he was the least confused about John Keats. So he chose him.

But, as Jaris rambled on in the essay, the word *gobbledygook* came to mind—meaningless words strung together just to fill the white space on the page. Jaris glanced around at his fellow students. Marko and his buddies were laughing and tossing wads of paper in the air. They had given up. Alonee was diligently working. She knew what she was doing. Jaris continued to write, trying to squeeze his brain for a few droplets of what he knew about Keats.

But Jaris knew he was doomed. The essay counted for half the test. Even if he got one hundred percent on the true/false and multiple-choice questions—and he knew he didn't—the essay would sink him like a stone.

As Jaris filed out after the test, he said to Alonee, "I'm a dead duck. I just flunked that test."

"Aw Jaris, you probably did better than you think," Alonee said.

"I did okay on the pin-the-tail-on-the-donkey questions, but the essay killed me. I forgot everything I ever knew about John Keats, and I didn't know that much to start with," Jaris said. "Old Pippin loves to flunk students. It's his only revenge. He hates his students and they hate him. Alonee, I'm gonna drop from an A minus in English to a D, I just know it. I saw all the names of those old poets, and they all swam together in my mind—Shelley, Keats, Tennyson, whoever. I remembered a few snippets from Keats, but not enough. He talked about autumn and apples and nuts, I think. Maybe I mistook Keats for somebody else. I tell you, I'm doomed!"

Alonee put her small, soft hand on Jaris's arm. "Don't do this to yourself, Jaris. You're horribilizing."

"Is that a word?" Jaris asked.

"I'm not sure, but it means thinking the very worst is going to happen all the time,"

Alonee said. "Maybe Mr. Pippin will let you do a book report or something to bring up your grade."

"Yeah, right," Jaris whined, "and maybe it'll snow on the fourth of July." Jaris noticed Marko and his friends laughing about the test across the parking lot. They didn't care. As long as they kept a C average, the coaches would take care of them. They were all athletes.

As Jaris started for home, he noticed Mr. Pippin clutching his briefcase, running to his car. His briefcase bulged with tests. Many teachers would require three or four days to correct so many tests, but Mr. Pippin would have them all done tomorrow. He would pore over each one, if it took all night, writing his scathing comments in red ink. It was the only time he had the upper hand. His pen was like a tiny stiletto, striking out at his enemies.

Nobody knew much about Mr. Pippin's private life except that he lived alone. He may have been a widower or a divorced man. Maybe he never married. Jaris thought that he had little personality, so what girl would have wanted him? For a brief, wild moment Jaris considered running into the teachers' parking lot and confronting Mr. Pippin. He might make an impassioned appeal for another chance to make up for the test. He could somehow make Pippin understand how important his A average was to him. But Jaris could see the little gray man sneering at him and telling him to take his chances with everybody else. So in the end Jaris watched the little gray car with the gray driver vanish down the street.

When Jaris got home from school, he saw Grandma Jessie's car parked in the driveway. "I don't need this," he said under his breath. "Not today of all days."

"Hello sweetheart," Grandma greeted him breezily. "I hope you had a wonderful day."

"He always does," Mom answered for Jaris in a proud voice. "Jaris is an excellent student."

Jaris stared at them—at his mother, who expected him to be as smart as she was when he probably was not, then at his grandmother, who was trying to break up his parents' marriage. He said, "I flunked my English test today." He felt ugly and angry, and he wanted his mother and his grandmother to stop smiling at him. They did.

"Well, I'm sure it was an unfair test," Grandma Jessie asserted promptly. "Some of those teachers are so incompetent that they don't know how to test properly."

"No," Jaris snapped. "It was an okay test. I was just too stupid to study right for it."

Mom looked shocked. "Don't call yourself 'stupid.' You're beginning to sound like your father and I hate that," she said.

"I didn't say I was stupid. I said I was too stupid to study for the test, and it has nothing to do with Pop, okay?" Jaris then stomped down the hall to his room. Then he stopped, turned around, and went back to the living room where Mom and Grandma Jessie were talking in animated tones. "Grandma, remember that school in Santa Barbara you said I should think about going to? You said I should think before I gave you an answer. Well, I have now. I'm not leaving Tubman. So thanks, but no thanks."

"Jaris," Mom said softly, "when you are all upset like you are right now, it is no time to make a big decision. So why don't you—"

"I won't go, Mom. That's it. There isn't anything to think about. Forget it," Jaris protested, before going back to his room. He could imagine what they were saying about him. He didn't care.

The darkness descended. He had flunked English. He wouldn't get the part of Sydney Carton in the play. He would never get to date Sereeta.

Just when you think you got it all made, it crashes around your head.

In the morning, Jaris steeled himself for the inevitable. English was his second class today. He sat through Ms. McDowell's history class without hearing much. He was dreading that walk to English and Mr. Pippin saying in his nasal voice, "Well, all the tests have been corrected, and as usual I am very disappointed."

Mr. Pippin came into the classroom with his shoulders straighter than usual. Jaris figured this was his favorite part of teaching English at Tubman High. Perhaps this was the only thing left that he enjoyed doing: getting even with the dunderheads and boors who made his life miserable.

When Mr. Pippin returned Marko Lane's paper, the football player made a paper airplane out of it to show his contempt. But Jaris saw the large red "F" before the test took flight. Mr. Pippin was on the warpath today. Usually even Marko made a D.

Mr. Pippin came down Jaris's aisle. He put Jaris's test paper down at the corner of his desk. Jaris could not bear to look at it. He turned it over, folded it, and stuck it in his binder. During class, Jaris finally worked up enough courage to pull the test out and look at it. He couldn't hide from the truth forever. He might as well know the worst.

Mr. Pippin wrote in his usual red ink across the top of the paper, "Well below your usual performance." His red criticisms were sprinkled throughout the essay.

The grade was B.

CHAPTER EIGHT

Jaris stared at the B in disbelief. He looked up at Mr. Pippin. The teacher was looking right at him. There was a strange, almost whimsical smile on Mr. Pippin's face. It was as if they both knew—Jaris and Mr. Pippin—that Jaris did not deserve the B. But every day Jaris came to class, dutifully took notes, and never joined in Pippin bashing, the class sport. Jaris was a good student. He flubbed this one test, but he was a good student and a good young man. Mr. Pippin decided to cut him some slack. So the grade was a gift of sorts, a gift that Jaris never expected.

And it would remain their secret, Jaris's and Mr. Pippin's. Jaris would now work

even harder in class to prove to Mr. Pippin
that his noble gesture had been right.

"How bad?" Alonee asked after class.

"You know, Alonee, you were right as
usual. I guess I did better than I thought. I
got a B," Jaris replied with a happy grin.

Alonee gave Jaris a playful punch. "You
dark dude, you. You really had me going!"

"Funny," Jaris thought. "I thought I
had Mr. Pippin all figured out, but I was
wrong." As beaten down and humiliated as
Mr. Pippin was by his students, he still
cared enough with a teacher's heart to bend
the rules for one boy who was trying. After
forty years of an increasingly hard struggle
against his own inadequacies, Mr. Pippin
still wanted to make a difference in a young
person's life.

When Jaris got home from school, he
told his mother he got a B in the test he
thought he'd flunked.

"Oh my goodness!" Mom exclaimed.
"That's great. But, you know, you were *so*
upset that I started feeling guilty. It made

me wonder if I'm putting too much pressure on you kids to do well. I don't want you to feel you have to make As all the time, Jaris."

"No, Mom," Jaris said, "I want the As for me. I know you want them too, but I'm doing it for me. All my life since I started school I wanted to do really good."

Mom smiled. "You're an overachiever like me. I was the same way in school. But, honey, even if you do flunk once in a while, it's not the end of the world. There are triumphs and failures for all of us," Mom said, a faintly sad look coming to her face. "Sometimes you think you're on top of the world. And then the earth starts shaking, and you realize it wasn't the top of the world after all. It was a volcano!"

Jaris wondered what Mom was thinking of. A pensive sorrow was in her eyes. Jaris hoped the volcano she was standing on was not her marriage to Pop.

Still revved up by the unexpected B from Mr. Pippin, Jaris decided to do something really bold. Even though he had no reason to expect her to say yes, he decided to ask Sereeta out on a date. He searched his mind for something spectacular to offer her. An ordinary movie would not do. A lame beach party was ridiculous. Sereeta liked music, so maybe he could get tickets to a really hot concert. Several big musicals were in town, and Sereeta said she liked musical productions—maybe *Phantom of the Opera*. Or maybe he could take her on a moonlight cruise on the bay.

Every time Jaris had thought of asking Sereeta Prince out on a date, he chickened out. He knew he would feel very bad if she turned him down. He kept turning the idea over and over in his mind. Should he risk the hurt and ask, or should he be a coward and never even know if she might have said yes?

At lunchtime on Wednesday, Jaris shared his dilemma with Trevor and Sami. "I'm trying to plan a great date with Sereeta, so when I ask her she's likely to want to go."

Sami laughed scornfully. "Girls don't go on dates with guys because they're gonna do something amazing," she said. "They go 'cause they like the dude."

"Yeah," Trevor agreed.

Jaris popped open his soft drink. "I still think it'd be good if I suggested something really cool," he said.

"I'd rather go to a boxing match with a boy I was crazy about than hang out at the hottest concert in town with somebody I didn't like. That'd be lame," Sami said.

Alonee joined the discussion. "If a boy lights your fire, you want to be with him, even if you're watching them recycle aluminum cans. Sami's right."

"Yeah, but I don't want to take her to some cheesy movie," Jaris complained. "I don't want her thinking I'm a nerd or something."

"You're thinking you've got to make up for something you don't have by making the date special," Alonee said. "But you've got a lot going for you, boy. You got those deep, dark eyes. You look kind of brooding and mysterious, and girls go for that. Maybe Sereeta's been hoping you'll ask her out."

Jaris laughed. "I don't think so, but thanks Alonee," he chuckled.

"You are pretty awesome in your own way, Jaris Spain," Alonee said. "Might be a lot of girls here at Tubman wishing you'd ask them for a date."

"If *I* like a boy, I ask him," Sami asserted. "I just grab the bull by the horns and ask that boy. If he says no, then he's the loser, right? 'Cause I'm hot."

"That works for you, Sami, 'cause you've got attitude, but it wouldn't work for me," Alonee said a little wistfully.

Trevor finished his tuna sandwich and made a face. He washed it down with a ginger ale. "Jaris, I think you're being a fool to even ask that girl. She's too hot for regular guys like us. When she comes in the classroom, all the guys are looking at her and she knows it. She knows they're drooling over her. I'm not holding it against the girl, but she's like a fifteen on a scale of one to ten."

"I hate that rating business," Sami said. "Like we're all eggs that go down a chute and got to be given a score. Everybody got a good side and a bad side. Maybe one dude's idea of a ten is somebody else's idea of a one."

"Sereeta's not stuck up," Jaris explained. "I know she's beautiful, but she's not stuck up. She's always really nice."

When Jaris went into American History I, he was sweating. He had decided to ask Sereeta today. He looked for her immediately, as he always did, but she wasn't in her usual place. Sereeta never missed class, and she wasn't tardy. But suddenly the door opened, and in rushed Sereeta with DeWayne Pike. "We made it," DeWayne gasped. "We beat the bell!" Sereeta looked at DeWayne and giggled.

Jaris's hopes sank. They had been together, Sereeta and DeWayne.

DeWayne was moving in on Sereeta. It was probably already a done deal. It would be ridiculous for Jaris to make his pitch for a date. Still, Jaris was going to try. He'd made up his mind to do it after class, and he'd hate himself if he just turned cowardly and went slinking off.

Jaris didn't focus on Ms. McDowell's lecture as much as he usually did, but he took notes. He kept plotting how he would get up quickly after the bell and follow Sereeta out. He needed to get to her before anybody else started a conversation with her.

When the bell rang ending class, Jaris almost fell over his own backpack, but he scrambled safely to Sereeta's side. Unfortunately, DeWayne was already there.

"I think seeing *Les Misérables* will help give us the flavor of the French Revolution and make the auditions easier," DeWayne was saying.

"That's a great idea," Sereeta said. "It's a wonderful musical anyway. I'm really looking forward to seeing it. I already have the music, and I just love it."

They continued walking along, talking, laughing. Jaris followed at a distance. He felt like a stray dog, hopefully trailing a possible friend. No way could he break into their conversation without seeming like a complete fool.

DeWayne slipped an arm around Sereeta's shoulders. It was like they were already dating. But maybe that was just DeWayne's way. He didn't necessarily have an interest in Sereeta besides wanting to play Sydney Carton opposite her as Lucie. He thought it would be good chemistry. Or maybe he *was* interested in her. What guy wouldn't be?

The bell rang for the next class. Jaris had missed his chance. He had to go to science and learn more about the disappearing species.

Jaris arrived home in a grumpy mood. Mom was on the computer, and Chelsea was heading for the door. "I'm riding my bike over to Sandra's house, Mom. We're going to be studying," she said.

"Okay," Mom replied. "Don't be late for dinner."

"Hi chili pepper," Jaris said as he passed his sister. Chelsea smiled, but she had a funny look on her face.

"Whasup?" Jaris asked her.

"Nothing," Chelsea almost snapped. "I'm going to Sandra's house. What's the big deal?"

Jaris watched his little sister go down the driveway. She was wearing her brand-new jeans, the ones that were so tight they looked as if they were painted on her. Jaris wondered why Chelsea was wearing those jeans to go to Sandra's house. Pop had not liked the jeans when Chelsea brought them home from a shopping trip with Mom.

"They're too tight, baby," he had told his daughter.

"Oh Pop," Chelsea had said, "all the girls are wearing them." Mom backed her up. Mom said even the little girls in her classroom were wearing them.

"It's the style," Mom had said.

"Oh well then, forgive me for questioning the tight jeans on my little girl," Pop had said with exaggerated respect. "Whatever is the style must be followed. It is the law. If the style requires that girls wear bikinis to school, so be it."

"Oh Lorenzo," Mom had laughed.

Jaris remembered that he had winced. Mom was always undermining Pop's authority. There was a secret understanding between Mom and the kids that Pop was woefully old-fashioned and that Mom's word was the rule.

Jaris watched Chelsea jump on her bike and snatch a quick look back at the house. Could she have wondered if anybody was watching her? Satisfied that nobody was, Chelsea did not turn left toward Sandra's house. She turned toward Grant Avenue. But Jaris was watching.

"Okay chili pepper, let's see what's going on," Jaris muttered to himself. Brandon Yates lived over near Grant. As she biked along, Chelsea was texting somebody.

Jaris got on his own bike and followed at a distance. He had a strong suspicion that his sister was meeting Brandon and some of his friends. Jaris didn't like the idea of Chelsea lying to Mom about where she was going. He didn't like her being with a Tubman student like Yates, a guy who was already in minor trouble at the school for ditching classes and then forging his dad's name to a note.

Jaris felt bad spying on Chelsea, but he knew he'd feel much worse if she got in over her head. He hung back at the top of a hill and watched Chelsea pull into the driveway of an apartment complex. Even at a distance, he could hear rap music blasting from the place. A party was going on.

When Chelsea went inside the apartment nearest to the street, Jaris came up behind the building. He could smell marijuana. Raucous voices and laughter came from the apartment. Jaris decided to make his move. He went to the door and knocked hard.

B.J. answered. He looked stoned. "Hey man," he mumbled to Jaris, "you come to party?"

Jaris looked past B.J. to where Brandon and Chelsea were drinking wine. "Hey, chili pepper," Jaris yelled, "this don't look much like Sandra's house."

Chelsea gasped. "Jaris! You followed me!"

"My bad," Jaris snapped. He shove Brandon aside and grabbed his sister's hand. He glared at Brandon and yelled in his face. "You leave my sister alone, you hear what I'm saying? She's in middle school, you creep!"

Jaris pulled Chelsea toward the door.

"We weren't doing anything wrong," Chelsea cried. "What's the matter with you, Jaris?"

Chelsea yanked on her hand, trying to break free of Jaris's grasp, but he held on. He pulled her out the door and into the parking lot. "You smoke any dope, girl?" he asked her harshly.

"No! I didn't," Chelsea said, beginning to cry. "I didn't do anything wrong. It was just a party!"

"B.J. is a drug dealer. You think it's okay for a middle school kid to be at a party with a drug dealer?" Jaris demanded.

"I don't know anything about him. I was there with Brandon." Tears streamed down her face, and she was shaking.

"How much of that cheap rotgut did you drink, girl?" Jaris asked her. Chelsea's eyes were wide and terrified. She had never seen her brother like this. She barely even recognized his voice, it was so harsh and angry.

"I just had a sip, I swear," Chelsea whispered. "Oh Jaris, are you going to rat me out to Mom and Pop?"

"Maybe." Jaris said. "Maybe you'll be grounded for the rest of the year. For sure you can kiss that cell goodbye. And you know the school trip your class is taking to the amusement park? We can axe that too as far as you're concerned."

Chelsea was shaking with sobs.

"Get on your bike, girl. We're going home," Jaris commanded.

CHAPTER EIGHT

Halfway home, Chelsea said in a trembling voice, "Jaris, I swear I'll never do anything like this again. Please don't tell Mom and Pop. They'll never trust me again."

"Why should they?" Jaris asked coldly from his bike. He was riding alongside Chelsea.

"Please Jaris. I swear I've learned my lesson. I was scared in there. I was sorry I'd come. Brandon said it was his parents' house, and we'd listen to some cool music and have pizza. When I got inside there were all those weird guys," Chelsea explained.

"Drug dealers, dropouts, slimy night crawlers who could eat up a kid like you and spit you out," Jaris said.

"Jaris, I swear I'll drop Brandon for-ever, and I won't *ever* lie about where I'm going. Honest. Just *please* don't rat me out," Chelsea pleaded fervently.

Jaris turned and looked at his sister. "Okay, chili pepper, but you are in such a

155

world of trouble if it happens again. I'm not kidding. You hear what I'm saying? I find that you text that creep one time and I'm blowing the whistle on you," he warned.

"I promise, I promise. I was scared, Jaris, I was looking for a way out even before you came. Oh thank you, Jaris, for not telling Mom and Pop. You won't be sorry. You won't *ever* be sorry," Chelsea said.

"I hope not," Jaris said, " 'cause if I am, *you'll* be sorrier."

At Tubman High the next day, Jaris resumed his mission to ask Sereeta for a date. But first he waited for Brandon Yates to get off the bus.

"Yates," Jaris shouted. Brandon walked over to where Jaris stood. He looked scared. Jaris was over six feet tall, and, though he was lean, he was muscular. He was a good head taller than Brandon. "Listen up, bro," Jaris said in his toughest street voice. "You so much as text my sister one more time, and I'll change your face. You hear what

I'm sayin'? I'm being straight with you, man. Don't you go near that girl *ever* again, or you'll be the sorriest dude in the 'hood. You get my meaning?"

"Yeah, sure. I don't even like her that much. I mean she's a flirt. She wears tight jeans and—" Brandon said. "She come on to me first."

"Okay, I don't care what stupid things she does. She doesn't know she's playing with fire. I'm not gonna let *nobody* ruin my sister's life, got it? Stay away from her, man," Jaris said.

"Got it, man," Brandon said. He hurried away then to join the stream of students going into Tubman.

Once again, Sereeta left American History I with some friends, and Jaris couldn't get to her. "Tomorrow," he told himself. "Nothing is going to stop me tomorrow."

When Jaris got home from school that night, he went on the computer in search of information about the Madagascar fish eagle. He noticed Chelsea was very busy with her own homework. After dinner, Jaris followed his father outside where he was puttering around his pickup truck.

"Reading *A Tale of Two Cities* every day?" Pop asked.

"You better believe it, Pop. I'm getting so close to Sydney Carton he's like my brother."

"You know," Pop went on, "I've been thinking. You know what you should do when you audition, Jaris?" A sly smile crossed Pop's face. He was really handsome when he smiled, but he didn't do it too often lately. "You need to wear the clothes of the period. The kind of clothes Sydney Carton wore. A kind of threadbare dark suit, trousers from the eighteenth century. You could get all you need in that costume store over on Pequot Avenue. Black suit, vest, the whole package."

"You don't think Mr. Wingate would think I was going overboard, do you?" Jaris asked.

"No. Here's something I never told you before, son. Twenty-five years ago, when I was in high school over at Hoover, Wingate was there too. He was only a couple years older than us. He was handsome, and he wanted to be an actor. He got some small roles, but he never got a hold of the brass ring. I remember he'd do all kinds of wild things to be noticed in an audition. He liked to say, 'Do what you can to get their attention and then act!'"

"Man," Jaris said, "I always thought Wingate was somebody who wanted to be an actor. That's a great idea, Pop. I'll bring the clothes to school and right before the audition I'll change. Man, I'm sure glad I asked you for help on this, Pop. You've been great."

"Well, the old grease monkey still has a few tricks up his sleeve," Pop said, grinning. "I'd really get a big kick out of it if you got the part, Jaris."

Jaris felt a slight cold chill go up his spine. Now that Pop was so into this project, if Jaris didn't get the part, it wouldn't be Jaris's disappointment alone. It would be another blow for Pop.

Jaris was almost asleep that night when he sensed someone in the room. He was startled to see his father, hovering over him. "Boy," Pop said, "don't forget the wig. You need a wig so you got hair like that dude Carton." Pop padded barefoot across the room and stuck some cash in Jaris's backpack. "This should cover it. Skip the change. The wig is important, though. Guys had long hair then, and they tied it sort of like in a ponytail with ribbons. You want a white shirt too. You can look at pictures of guys in the American Revolutionary era. Both revolutions came around the same time."

In the dark, Pop was grinning. His bright, white teeth glowed. He was really into this. "Oh, and one more thing, son. Don't tell a soul at school about the plan. Not even your best friend. It's just between you and me, right?"

CHAPTER NINE

Right, Pop," Jaris said.

"Oh, and don't even tell your mom. You know how her mother is. For sure Mom would tell Grandma and then you might as well put it on a billboard," Pop said.

"You got it," Jaris said.

Jaris would have liked to share his plan with Alonee, and he was sure she wouldn't tell anybody else, but he respected his father's wishes.

When Alonee and Sereeta showed up together for lunch at school, Jaris made his move. "Hey Sereeta," Jaris greeted her in a shaky voice. "How's it going?"

"Pretty good," she replied. "I'm still reading *A Tale of Two Cities* for the auditions."

"Me too," Jaris said. His mouth was very dry. "Uh, you busy this weekend, Sereeta?"

Sereeta shrugged. "Not especially. Why?"

"I thought maybe you'd like to go somewhere on Saturday night maybe," Jaris said. His mouth was drier. His voice sounded squeaky, like it could use some oil. He steeled himself for the rejection.

"Sure, that'd be fun," Sereeta responded.

Jaris's heart was racing. He couldn't believe Sereeta had actually said yes.

"So where would you like to go?" Jaris asked.

"Oh, I'd like to see a very funny movie," Sereeta replied. "That's what I'd like more than anything. Then get some of those new shrimp tacos at Julio's. That's right by the big theater at the mall. I so need to see a funny movie. There's so much to be gloomy about that I want to laugh until my sides ache."

"Yeah, I like funny movies too," Jaris agreed. "Great. I only got a provisional driver's license, so Trevor's older brother can drop us off at the mall."

"Fine," Sereeta said.

Jaris was shaking all over and hoping he didn't show it. He was still shaking when he went to his science class and listened to Mr. Buckingham bewailing the disappearing lowland gorillas. Right at this moment Jaris did not care about the endangered species. He was going on a date with Sereeta Prince, something he never believed would happen. It was as unlikely in his mind as watching a UFO land and being invited to dinner by the aliens. Mr. Buckingham said the bees were vanishing. Jaris only knew he was taking Sereeta out on Saturday night. The plight of the bees would have to wait. The plants were not getting pollinated, Mr. Buckingham said. Jaris only knew he had to find a really great funny movie for Saturday night with Sereeta.

On his way home from school, Jaris stopped at the costume store.

"I need to dress like a French guy in the late 1700s, the time of the French Revolution," Jaris told the clerk. "I need a white shirt, dark trousers, a coat, and it can be crummy looking. I need boots. And I need a wig. I guess guys had ponytails that they tied with ribbons in those days."

"You're in business," the clerk said. He rounded up everything Jaris needed for well under the amount of money Pop had given him. Jaris tried everything on to make sure it fit. He needed to use a belt to tighten the trouser waist a little, but it worked. Jaris was amazed at how different the period clothing made him look. He didn't look like a teenager anymore. He looked like a young man, maybe in his late twenties. Pop was right. Dressing like this would add power to his audition.

When Jaris got home from the costume shop, he cornered Chelsea. "Chili pepper, I need to know what the funniest movie around is. I'm taking Sereeta out on

Saturday night, and she wants to see a really funny movie."

"You're going on a date with Sereeta?" Chelsea cried. She jumped up and high-fived Jaris. "Way to go, bro!"

"I know you're a funny movie freak, chili pepper, so steer me right," Jaris said.

"*Shipwreck*," Chelsea said. "It's about these two stupid guys who ditch a yacht on an island. It's so hilarious Sandy and I almost choked on our popcorn."

Jaris got suggestions from Alonee, Trevor, and Sami too. Finally he settled on a movie about a newlywed couple. Everything that could happen upset their wedding and their honeymoon. It was titled *Wedding-Schmedding*.

Sereeta and her family lived in the nicest part of the neighborhood, as far from Grant Avenue as possible. The yard was cleverly landscaped with plants that needed little or no water. "My stepfather is a land-scaper," Sereeta explained. "He got rid of all our petunias and geraniums."

"Looks good," Jaris commented.

"I miss the petunias," Sereeta sighed.

Trevor's brother dropped them at the mall, and, as they walked toward the theater, Sereeta said, "My mom is having a baby."

"Yeah?" Jaris said. He vaguely remembered when Chelsea came along. He was only a toddler. But he liked her. She was fun to watch. He became very protective of her when he was about four. "I bet you're excited." The words were out before Jaris had time to think about them. He knew almost at once that he shouldn't have said them. Sereeta went through such a painful period when her parents divorced. Now her mother was newly married to her stepfather. And the pair was having a baby, *their* baby. Sereeta would be an outsider. Her mother and her stepfather would form a unit around the new child.

"I guess it's exciting to have a new baby in the house," Sereeta finally replied. "My mom is really thrilled. She's only thirty-five, but she wasn't sure she could have another child. It'll be my stepfather's first child. So it's a big deal," Sereeta smiled. It was not a happy smile. It was a forlorn smile. "I wish I could take a long vacation or something when the baby comes home, you know, let them have their space."

"Maybe you could spend time with your father," Jaris suggested.

"He married again too. His new wife has two kids. They're active little boys. I don't fit in there," Sereeta explained. "You know, once I saw a documentary on TV about, you know, some commune or something. All the kids were raised by all the mothers and fathers, and they didn't bond with anybody special. It sounds weird, but I think I'd like that better. Then I wouldn't, you know, miss Dad . . . or miss Mom even when she's there." Sereeta laughed dryly. "Listen to me. We're on our way to see a funny movie and I'm getting all melodramatic!"

"I polled all my friends to find the funniest movie, Sereeta, and this is it," Jaris said as they turned into the theater. He could understand Sereeta's pain. Just thinking about his parents ever splitting up made him crazy. He felt so sorry for her. He hoped the movie was really, *really* funny.

They found a seat in the center of the theater and shared a bag of popcorn. Jaris was overjoyed when Sereeta started laughing early in the movie. It was clever and funny, and there were honest-to-goodness belly laughs throughout the movie. A new young comedian starred in it, and the reviews were saying he was a younger version of Jim Carrey and a new edgier Chris Rock.

"I loved it," Sereeta enthused as they walked to the taco restaurant. "I haven't laughed so much in ages. I've seen the guy who played Jason on TV. He is so funny."

There was a small waterfall in the patio of the restaurant. Colored lights played on the spray of water.

CHAPTER NINE

"Pretty, huh?" Sereeta asked. "Most malls don't have little touches like that. I think it's important. A little drop of beauty in a bland place. It lifts the spirits. They do better in that way in Europe. They're more people friendly." Sereeta smiled then. "The taco is good too. You know, I've never been out of the United States, except to Mexico a couple times, but I'd like to visit France. Wouldn't you, Jaris?"

"Yeah, I guess," Jaris said, though he'd never given it much thought. He didn't know anybody who had been to Europe.

"I'd like to go to the little cafés in France, and to that big cathedral with the stained glass windows. They say it's like walking into heaven or something. The different colors just surround you," Sereeta said. "I mean you'd *have* to be happier there, wouldn't you?"

"I don't know," Jaris responded. "Now that I'm reading *A Tale of Two Cities* I'm thinking it's not the place where you live that makes you happy, but it's you. Like

Sydney Carton. He's so sad and down on himself, and he's there in that great city, and he's smart—"

"Yeah," Sereeta agreed. "He's sitting around getting drunk in all those quaint little cafés. He calls himself 'a dissolute dog.' But he's got a great heart. Down deep he's nobler than most people." A strange look came to Sereeta's face then. "Jaris, wouldn't it be awesome if we both got parts in that play and then someday, years from now, we had dinner in a little café in Paris and reminisced about it all. We've got to promise each other right now that, whatever happens, we will meet at a little café in Paris someday and just talk."

"Yeah," Jaris said, "it's a deal."

They had their tacos. As they walked toward the parking structure where Trevor's brother waited, Sereeta said, "I had a good time tonight, Jaris. Thanks for asking me. I loved the movie, and it was cool being with you."

"Thanks for agreeing to go with me, Sereeta," Jaris said. "I had a really great time too."

When they arrived at Sereeta's house, Jaris walked her to the door. "Nobody's home. My mom and stepfather are having dinner with friends. They go out a lot. Mom says, after the baby comes, life will change. So while they're free, they want to do things."

"Well," Jaris said as she opened the front door. "Here we are."

"Thanks again for tonight," Sereeta said.

"Yeah, it was wonderful," Jaris told her, turning to walk back to the car. Sereeta stopped him with a hand on his shoulder. She gently turned him toward her and placed both hands on his shoulders. Jaris leaned down to kiss her. She put her hands around his neck and kissed him back. Then she turned and went inside.

On the way home, Jaris berated himself for not asking for another date. The night had gone so well. Jaris felt good about it. He should have asked, and yet maybe not. There was time—time to savor tonight and build on it. He always knew he loved Sereeta, but he never realized her depths. She was not only beautiful, but she was easy to talk to. She had confided in him. She gave him the compliment of opening her heart to him.

When Jaris came to work at the Chicken Shack on Sunday, Sami and some friends came in. "So how did you do, man?" Sami asked.

Jaris smiled. "We had a great time. She's even more wonderful than I imagined," he said.

"Oh, he got it bad," Sami laughed.

At school on Monday, Marko Lane sneered as Jaris and Trevor walked by. "Some chicks will go out with anybody," Marko said loud enough for Jaris to hear. "Some chicks so boy crazy they'd go out with a monkey on a stick." Jaris and Trevor ignored them and walked on.

As Jaris was eating lunch with Alonee and Trevor, DeWayne came along. "So, you polishing up your Sydney Carton, Jaris?" he asked.

"Yeah," Jaris admitted, "studying like crazy."

"Me too," DeWayne chimed in. "That Carton is a great role. Sort of like Heathcliffe in *Wuthering Heights*. I did that role. A dark and brooding man."

"How come you don't want to play Charles Darnay?" Alonee asked. "He gets all the romantic scenes."

Sami laughed. "That dude Dickens, he didn't write no good romantic scenes. When Darnay and Lucie are together, it's all so stuffy that it makes me howl."

"Carton is more interesting," DeWayne asserted. "He's the hero."

"That's true," Sami agreed. "If I get to do Miss Pross I can grab old DeFarge and fight her to the death. I end up killing her. She tears at my face and everything, but I don't let go and finally I get her gun and—pop—she's a goner. That wicked old woman is history!"

Alonee laughed. "You'd make a great Miss Pross, Sami. I don't see how they can give it to anybody else!" she said.

When Jaris got home, Greg Maynard's car was in the driveway again. Pop had gone up north to visit his sister for a day. She was having back surgery. Jaris thought it was strange that Maynard would be here just now. Did Mom tell him when the coast was clear? Jaris felt guilty thinking like that, but he couldn't help it.

Mom and Maynard were laughing as Jaris came in. They sounded like friends, not principal and teacher. Their voices were light and playful.

"Did she really say that?" Mom asked in mock horror.

"She did," Maynard replied. "I was quite astonished. Her exact words were 'the entire program seems to have been written by a slightly educated chimpanzee!'" Laughter gurgled in Maynard's voice.

"Oh my goodness!" Mom exclaimed. "She is so out of touch with current educational philosophy."

"Thankfully, retirement looms for the poor old dear," Maynard said. "She must be sixty-five if she's a day."

"Actually she's only sixty-four," Mom giggled.

"Oh good heavens, then we'll have her for another year," Maynard gasped.

Jaris stood unseen at the door at the side of the house. He wanted to burst in and give them both dirty looks, but he remained there in silence listening.

"Do you want more coffee, Greg?" Mom asked.

"Yes, thank you. With all your other talents, you do make the best coffee I have ever tasted," Maynard oozed.

"I put in almond-flavored creamer," Mom said. "My secret weapon."

"Well, it's great coffee," Maynard said.

"I made some macaroons. Want to try one?" Mom offered.

Maynard beamed at Mom. "Of course. Macaroons are favorites of mine."

"I don't cook much, but they're so easy to just mix and drop on the cookie sheet," Mom explained.

Mom didn't sound like she usually sounded. She sounded like a girl at Tubman High, a silly, flirting girl. Jaris broke into a cold sweat. Jaris wondered if this was how it started before Sereeta's parents broke up. Had there been somebody in her mother's life who seemed much more attractive than Sereeta's father?

Jaris's clenched fists swung at his sides, hitting his thighs. He was frightened, angry, frustrated. He didn't know what to do.

"Well, another home run," Maynard commented. "A perfect macaroon."

Jaris couldn't go inside. He couldn't bear to greet Mom as if everything was all right. He couldn't be civil to this man who came here like a thief in the night when

Pop was gone. Jaris was afraid he would say something awful, something he might regret.

Jaris went instead to the woodpile that Pop was slowly building for winter warmth. Every few days he went out and chopped more logs for the fireplace.

Jaris had to do something physical to let out his emotions. With every blow of the axe, he felt the anger ease a bit. But deep down there was a raw wound. Mom liked Greg Maynard. And he liked her. That was obvious. That didn't mean Mom wanted to leave Pop and be with Maynard. But she was often disgusted with Pop, and she might be comparing him with Maynard who was cool and charming. Maynard was more like Mom than Mom was like Pop. If Grandma Jessie could have chosen a husband for Mom, he probably would have been a lot like Greg Maynard.

Greg Maynard made pleasant small talk. Mom liked that. She was always telling Pop that he was too quiet. Sometimes she was lonely.

"You're as much company as that rubber plant," she complained to Pop after one of his long silences.

Jaris had never chopped so much wood so fast. He worked like a madman. From the corner of his eye he saw Maynard at the door leading to the backyard. Maynard stood there a moment. Then he opened the door and said, "Well, that's quite a pile of firewood. You guys will be all set come winter."

Jaris glared at the man. He made no effort to be cordial. "Whatever," Jaris said in his coldest, most unfriendly voice. He wanted to make it clear to Greg Maynard that a sullen, evil-tempered teenager came with Mom. Part of the package would be dealing with Jaris.

CHAPTER TEN

Greg Maynard persisted, though. He stood there in the doorway and said, "Well Jaris, your mother and I got a lot of important work done tonight. She's a wonderful teacher and a real asset to the school. She's been a big help in putting together this new program."

Jaris noticed that Greg Maynard looked less cheerful than he did moments ago. Jaris continued to glare at him. "Whatever," Jaris replied, taking another swing at the wood with the axe.

Jaris figured Maynard wanted to tell him how his mother spoke proudly of her bright son. He wanted to butter Jaris up, but Jaris was spoiling his plans. Jaris was making a friendly conversation impossible.

"Well, I have to go," Maynard said, clutching his briefcase and hurrying to his car as if he were escaping something unpleasant. Jaris smiled to himself. Might as well let the creep know what he was getting into, Jaris thought.

Jaris knew how it was supposed to go when people got divorced and blended families were created. It was supposed to be nice and smooth, and everybody just got along. But it wasn't that way. Jaris wanted his family unbroken. He didn't want the pain Sereeta was dealing with. And he hoped Greg Maynard was shocked and worried as he scurried away.

Mom came outside shortly after Maynard left. "Hi sweetie," she greeted him. "You've really been working here, haven't you? We have enough wood for two winters."

"Yeah," Jaris mumbled.

Mom came closer. "Is everything all right, Jaris? You looked worried," she said.

"You get all your work done with that guy, Mom, or is he coming back? You sure seemed to be having a good time yakking in there with him. I bet you never thought teaching school could be so much fun." Jaris was shaking with anger, and his voice came out unevenly.

"What in the world is wrong with you, Jaris?" Mom asked. "We did get a lot accomplished."

"Who said anything was wrong, Mom?" Jaris asked coldly. "Or maybe the guilty need no accuser, or so they say."

"What a foul thing to say, Jaris," Mom said. She looked tense then. "You didn't say anything to Mr. Maynard, did you? You weren't rude to him, were you? Remember, he's my principal. His evaluation of me is important to my career."

"He kept trying to make small talk, Mom, and I just said 'whatever.' I'm not "good at small talk, Mom. I'm like Pop. We're not charming big talkers like Maynard, who can yak for hours and hours about nothing," Jaris said.

"Jaris, you are being very impossible. You act as if I had a date with Mr. Maynard. We are working on a very important project to improve student achievement. Of course, it makes it easier that he's a nice person, easy to work with. Everyone enjoys working with personable people. What is sinister about that?" Mom said.

Chelsea came in then. "Hi Mom, hi Jaris. Keisha came up with a cool new cheer. We worked late on our routine." Chelsea looked from her mother to her brother. "What's the matter? Did something bad happen?"

"No," Mom said quickly. "I just had a long, hard meeting with my principal and I'm tired. Look at all the wood Jaris chopped. Your father will be so happy."

Everyone auditioning for *A Tale of Two Cities* was asked to come to the auditorium on Friday. Jaris was surprised that so many kids were trying out.

"Remember now," Mr. Wingate explained, "if you do not get the role you want, you can still work on the play. We will need people for wardrobe, tickets, lights, sound, making scenery, publicity, everything. Do not be prima donnas. This play was adapted from a very complex book, and we all have our work cut out for us."

Mr. Wingate then introduced the New York playwright who made the adaptation. "We are honored to have Ms. Jeannie Duvall here with us for the auditions," he said. She was a striking woman of about thirty, tall and willowy, with her black hair severely pulled back in a ponytail.

"On Monday afternoon," Mr. Wingate went on to say, "Ms. Duvall and I, with the help of two college professors from the drama departments of the university, will judge auditions for the lesser roles. On Tuesday afternoon we shall audition students for the major roles. Results of the auditions will be made known on Wednesday here in the auditorium. On Thursday we shall be signing up people to help in the production in other capacities."

Jaris felt numb. It was really happening. This was it. He hurried over to read who else was trying out for Sydney Carton. There were four other boys. Except for DeWayne, Jaris didn't know the others.

Alonee was waiting outside the auditorium. "When is the big day, Jaris?"

"On Tuesday I audition. On Wednesday we find out who got it. Man, I'm not going to sleep a wink until Wednesday. I don't see how I can even keep food down!" Jaris felt sick already. "Alonee, I can't believe I'm even doing this. I never acted before. What makes me think a nerd like me can pull it off?" he asked.

"You're not a nerd. You have a wonderful voice. It gives me chills when you speak from the stage. You look good too. And you've been rehearsing so much," Alonee assured him. "I believe you'll get it."

Jaris looked at the girl and smiled. "My little one-girl fan club," he said. In the fading light of the day, Jaris noticed how beautiful Alonee was with her little oval face, her big, expressive eyes, and her lovely full lips. She was such a good friend too. He couldn't believe how she was always there for him. "Alonee, you are my angel," he told her.

Alonee laughed. "I just have a feeling this might be your destiny, Jaris," she said.

"Alonee, everybody I know in this school likes you. You're a good friend and a good student. What's your destiny?" Jaris asked.

"I don't know. Mom tells me to do what makes me happy. Mom is raising four kids while Daddy works as a fireman. Mom is happy just staying home with her kids, and Daddy is happy being a fireman. My family is pretty cool. I want to find a place in the world like they have. I'm just not sure what kind of a place that'll be or what I'll be doing," Alonee said.

Jaris thought that, of all his friends, Alonee and Sami had the happiest families.

Pop got home Friday night from his sister's house. Jaris ran up to the pickup before he turned off the engine. "How's Aunt Lita?" he asked.

"She's doing fine," Pop said. "Came through like a trooper. She's got a long rehab, but she'll do fine. Her husband and kids are there for her."

"I audition Tuesday, Pop. It all comes down to Tuesday. Then we get the verdict on Wednesday," Jaris said.

Mom came out then. "Lorenzo, how's your sister?"

"She's doing fine. Can't keep a good girl down. Hey Monie, our actor here, he auditions on Tuesday," Pop said.

"Can the family come?" Mom asked.

"Not on Tuesday, but you can come for the results on Wednesday," Jaris said.

"Remember now, Jaris, the important thing is you did your best. We think you're wonderful if you get to play that Sydney Carton or not," Mom said.

Pop looked at Jaris, reached over and gave him a hug. "You're gonna win, boy. I'm standing right here now, looking at Sydney Carton," he assured Jaris.

"Well, I hope you get the role, sweetie," Mom added, "but don't be too disappointed if you don't. I missed being homecoming queen in high school even though I had my heart set on it. Now, looking back on it, it seems so trivial."

"This is different," Jaris said to her. To himself he said, "Homecoming queen *is* trivial. Playing Sydney Carton is major. It's important, really important."

Jaris spent the whole weekend going over the parts of the play he would do at the audition. He would do the dramatic quote at the end of the play, but also a scene where a bitter Carton has a poignant encounter with Lucie Manette. In that scene, he pledges to do anything for her or for someone she loved, and he would ask nothing in return. Jaris stood before the mirror and said, "I would embrace any sacrifice for you and for those dear to you."

A third scene Jaris would do had Carton seated at a table surrounded by liquor bottles, smiling drunkenly and shouting, "I am a disappointed drudge, sir. I care for no man on earth, and no man on earth cares for me."

Jaris had put on the clothes he got from the costume store to use during these final rehearsals. As he finished a scene, his door opened, and Chelsea stood there staring at her brother. "Jaris! You look awesome," she gasped.

"Don't you tell a soul about the costume, chili pepper," Jaris warned.

"I won't, but you look amazing!" Chelsea exclaimed. "And you sound great."

On Tuesday afternoon, the Miss Pross audition was first. Sami was shaking when she went in but screaming with excitement when she came out. "I think I got it! I think

I got it! Oh Jaris, listen to what I'm saying. When you audition, look right at that Lady Jeannie Duvall—eyeball to eyeball. If she likes you, you got it. Mr. Wingate, he's got the hots for her and he's gonna listen to her."

Jaris ducked into the restroom and donned his eighteenth-century costume. When he appeared on stage, there was a gasp. Jaris did not dare look at Mr. Wingate for fear of seeing a scornful look of disapproval. Jaris quickly arranged his first props, the liquor bottles. He sat down before them and cried out, with all the anguish he could muster, "Bring me another pint of this same wine!" He turned in the chair and looked right at the judges, hissing, "I am a disappointed drudge, sir. I care for no man on earth and no man on earth cares for me!" On fire with nervous energy, Jaris did the scene with Lucie Manette, pledging his devotion. His voice rising, Jaris cried, "There is a man who would give his life, to keep a life you love beside you. Farewell! A last God bless you!"

Then, finally, Jaris poured his baritone into the final scene, his eyes on the judges. He noticed that Jeanee Duvall stared, unblinking at him.

"It is a far, far better thing I do, than I have ever done; it is a far, far better rest I go to than I have ever known."

Jaris used his last drop of energy to flee behind the curtain. He vaguely heard another boy beginning his audition. He was bathed in his own perspiration. He was shaking.

No applause greeted the auditions. The judges quietly judged. Their reactions and decisions would wait for Wednesday.

Chelsea, Mom, and Pop joined Jaris in Mom's sedan for the ride down to the school on Wednesday afternoon. The results would be announced at five o'clock.

Mom kept telling Jaris not to be disappointed. Chelsea was too excited to speak. Pop kept grinning at Jaris and giving him the high sign.

Jaris felt as if he, like Sydney Carton, was going to his own execution.

He could not believe he might actually get the part. The dark fears that trailed him gathered and became deep and almost blinding. A small voice insisted to him that such good fortune could not come his way.

Sami Archer was chosen as Miss Pross. Sereeta was picked for Lucie Manette.

"And for the role of Sydney Carton," intoned Mr. Wingate, "we have chosen Jaris Spain."

The crowd melted before Jaris's tears. Mom kissed him. Pop kissed him. Chelsea kissed and hugged him. The family made their way out into the parking lot. It was almost dark now, but the moon was rising. Suddenly Jaris realized he was alone. His parents were gone. And then he saw them. They were dancing in the parking lot. Pop lifted Mom off her feet and they fell, laughing into each other's arms.

Jaris felt like he was finally outrunning the darkness.